JESUS OF GRAMOVEN

JESUS OF GRAMOVEN

Antonio Pérez Esclarín

Translated by Dinah Livingstone

ORBIS BOOKS

Maryknoll, New York 10545

Library of Congress Cataloging in Publication Data

Pérez Esclarín, Antonio.
    Jesus of Gramoven.

    I. Title.
PZ4.P4385Je   [PQ8550.26.E64]   863   79-22085
ISBN 0-88344-228-0

English translation of the Spanish *Jesús de Gramovén* copyright © 1980 by Orbis Books, Maryknoll, NY 10545

CONTENTS

WEDNESDAY IN HOLY WEEK

I

JESUS WAS HEART-SORE, struck by anguish as a man might be struck by a hurled rock. Before him at the church entrance was the Christ-statue, head on hand, with plaster face and unseeing eyes staring unblinkingly at the people who confided to him all their hopes and fears. It was the boredom in the statue's expression, boredom oblivious or impervious to human need, that made Jesus' blood run cold.

St. Teresa's Church was packed—women, men, children. Some of them, mostly the children, were in purple tunics. They pressed forward, blindly following those in front of them toward the great voiceless summons of the Nazarene. Some of the mothers held their children high to see better, and their tired, sweating faces mirrored the strain. Police and firemen lined the walls as if glued there, looking very serious and conscientious. There was music, oppressive over the heat of the close-packed crowd. And out in front, amid lamps and flowers bent under the cross, walking without moving above the murmuring crowd, was the Nazarene of St. Paul.

Jesus felt an extra hard shove, and turned round. A child's eyes were looking at him, and he wanted to smile.

"We must pray to him, you see. He fell down under the cross, he did. The Pharisees wanted to kill him," the mother was telling the wide-eyed child.

"Move along please, move along," called an usher, sounding authoritative from out of his ashy whiskers.

The crowd sweated and sighed in its slow advance toward the Nazarene.

3

The organ music seemed to intensify the heat. Some young men tried to push through the crowd, without asking permission, jingling the money in their small baskets. And suddenly from the middle of the church singing began, loud and tuneless, and almost every voice joined in:

> who givest both thy body and blood
> to the faithful soul as heavenly food,
> to the faithful soul as heavenly food.

> I confess with shame I am unfit
> to receive Holy Communion.

Jesus looked admiringly at the woman beside him. Where did she find the strength to sing so lustily in all this heat and with the weight of the small child asleep against her breast.

He moved forward with the other bodies, catching a momentary glimpse of a young priest at the high altar bright red and sweating under his heavy vestments as he gave communion. Beside him the candles shuttered in the dusty air.

"We see this stuff in the movies," said a child, pointing to one of the stations of the cross.

"Of course," agreed his mother.

A fireman was trying to carry out a fainting child. "Excuse me! Coming through!" he cried. His face had assumed, unconsciously, a hero's expression, and as he struggled through the crowd, people looked at the child's glazed eyes, dark against the sickly whiteness of his face.

A diminutive woman was carrying her two tiny children dressed in purple tunics in her arms.

Jesus wanted to think but could not. The crowd carried him toward the Nazarene.

"Look at him. You can see him from here."

"Poor thing."

"The Jews killed him."

"They beat him something awful, poor thing."

"And he was so good."

"Tomorrow we'll see him from the other side." The speaker's face was alight. Jesus thought, at first, it was from joy, but then he was not so sure.

"The Mass is ending. Let us ask the Nazarene to have mercy on us all. Let us pray."

When he spoke in his liturgical voice the priest became unintelligible. The Nazarene was nearer now, as the crowd pressed blindly forward.

"Let's get out. Come on, Carmen, the kid is fainting. Look at him, how white he's getting."

"You go, Mama, I want to see the Nazarene."

"If we split up we'll lose each other. Come on, he's fainting! He needs air."

"Wait for me at the door. I want to see him, now that I've gotten this far. . . . "

The Christ-statue did not look at the people. Wrapped in silence, it walked on above the crowd. The thin body was wrapped in a gold and purple cloak and grasped in its shining hands a polished cross covered with metal squares. Thus it advanced, painlessly, immobile in its artificiality, walking above the noisy multitude whose hands reached out to touch it and be sanctified. For the Christ-statue carried the cross, above history, above them. They were the crucified, after centuries still hoping. Wanting to hope.

The Roman soldier stopped a moment to wipe the sweat off his face. The heat was godawful. The sun beating down turned the slopes of Golgotha the color of unquenchable thirst. Voices were reaching him from the crowd below that was accompanying this visionary Jew lurching along under the weight of the cross. Maybe he wouldn't make it alive. Maybe he'd fall under the cross onto the dust and stones, and they would have to drag corpse and cross together up Golgotha and crucify a dead man. For days the stench of putrid flesh would reach Jerusalem and remind these repulsive Jews that Roman power and Roman laws were no joke.

The soldier smiled, a complacent smile that changed to a grimace of hatred as the mob came in sight. They were coming up the hill at a run, heedless of the sun and the stones, to get good places for the show. They were frenzied for the sight of blood and the sound of the death rattle. It was beyond him why they should want the death of one of their own, why they should have demanded it that very morning in voices shaking with hatred. They were impossible to understand. They had left off conspiring against Rome to demand of Rome the death of one of their own. What did these Jews really want? Everyone knew they hated Rome, but before Pilate they had clamored their loyalty. They must hate this poor convict even more than Rome. It was a fierce hatred that would make them cheer for Caesar. But what made them hate this fellow so much, when a few days ago they had received him so enthusiastically? Didn't we have to break up a wild demonstration only four or five days ago, when half of Jerusalem had gone out to greet him with branches and palms? Definitely the Jewish people were impossible to understand—unstable, fickle as whores, and therefore condemned to eternal subjection to the great Roman Empire.

This thought made the soldier swell with satisfaction. Refreshed, he continued up the hill.

At the top the post holes were ready. Frowning, he dispersed the curious onlookers, then drove the butt end of his lance into the new central hole and sat down on a stone to wait. He saw the sun-bleached bones remaining from old crucifixions. You would think these wretched Jews would finally learn! Always lying in wait like snakes to strike against Rome, too stupid to see that Rome was invincible. They and their useless, invisible, impotent God who never did a thing for them, but did that ever stop their besotted yammering by the Wailing Wall?. . . The soldier stared at a Jew just to test the power of a Roman gaze. The Jew looked back at him for only a few seconds, then looked away, as though he had only just noticed the parched hillside and found it fascinating. The soldier flushed and smiled with gratification. No one can outstare a Roman. No one. Except *of course the poor visionary, who this morning, even after his beating, had looked calmly and penetratingly into the eyes of Pilate himself. Pilate had probably condemned him more for that look of his than for all the yelling crowd demanding his death. So who was this Jew? Apart from his being a fanatic, there was no doubt that he was very brave. Never made a sound when the scourge laid open his shoulders or afterward when the guards knocked him around a bit. Not even when they crowned him—with a wreath of thorns—to while away the time. A king! King of the Jews! With a crown of thorns and a hollow reed for a scepter. A puppet king, a madman, who neither screamed nor raged when he was beaten, only looked at you with eyes that made you feel like you were beating a helpless child. Yes, he was mad, with his talk of another kingdom and his dreams of a world ruled by love. Deluded, ridiculous. . . .To think that these greasy Jews were the equal of Romans. . . . To think it and to say it with his eyes so plainly that Pilate himself had lost his self-possession, even shown a flash of fear.*

The soldier stood up. The mob-noise was coming closer. He saw the cross wavering and swaying. Yes, he'd wait for him and look at him with a Roman look and make him know before he died what a delusion his life had been.

Jesus turned his eyes from the Nazarene to the Dolorosa, a statue with a dead-white, European face, bloodless with dry pain. He thought of his mother, Maria, and felt again the anguish in his heart. She would be in her little house, or maybe following some procession, but wherever, she'd be praying "God and the Virgin" to take care of her son, Jesus. Since the second time he'd been fired, and especially since that night when some men had beaten him up, she couldn't sleep well. She woke up, calling his name, at the slightest sound. She had aged very quickly, and when he was home her fearful eyes were always following him, beseeching him wordlessly, burdening him.

"Don't worry, Mama. Nothing's going to happen to me,"

Jesus told her. "I'm not worrying." She pulled a smile over her dark face that showed her distress even more plainly.

"You know I'll be all right," Jesus insisted. "I'm only trying for a scrap of justice, Mama. To make 'our glorious constitution' a little bit true instead of one big lie. Why should a country like ours have hungry children, people without work, people working for starvation wages?. . . Why should rich kids be turned into mindless idiots stuffed with TV and fashion magazines? It makes me burn, Mama. That's why I have to keep trying to change things."

"I know, son, I know. . . . That's why I worry. Because that's why they'll put you in prison, or make you disappear one night, or put a bullet through you when no one's looking. The way you're going, my son, there's no room for you in Venezuela. There's no one else who thinks like you do."

Jesus made his way through the crowd into a corner of the church. There were some women with children there before him, and he stayed, wanting to think, but the ugly scar on the face of one of the children made him forget what he had wanted to think about. He saw another small, very clean Christ, hanging from wires in the center of the church. And beneath this Christ a voice was raised above the noise of the crowd:

"Brothers, let's all have a bit more silence in honor of our dear Nazarene of St. Paul. And we are all going to hear the word of God. Because it won't be me speaking. We are going to hear the words of Christ himself, written down for us by St. Matthew in chapter 16. Here Christ says to us: 'If any man would come after me, let him deny himself and take up his cross and follow me.' Brothers, being a Christian doesn't mean coming to church, doesn't mean kissing the medals on the Nazarene. It means hearing the word of God and doing it. And his word is quite plain. Every day each one of us must take up our own cross and nail ourselves to it on the Golgotha of our own lives. It means being patient with our poverty, enduring it without despair, because suffering detaches us from earthly things. Earth is suffering, and we are purified by our tears. Let us therefore go with the Nazarene, who called the poor blessed and suffered his own pain and hardship without complaint. In this way, as St. Paul says, 'We fill up what is wanting in the passion of Christ.' As gold is purified in the crucible, the soul is purified in suffering. We should not mind if we suffer. We should not mind if we are poor. We should rather rejoice. Because thus we are with Christ, thus we go with the Nazarene on his painful journey to Calvary. Let us remember that God himself did not give his mother riches and joy, but poverty and suffering. And her heart pierced by seven swords is the clearest proof that if we accept our suffering, we are with Christ."

Jesus wanted to scream. When had this priest ever suffered? He looked like he led a very comfortable life. When had he ever felt the burning sun, cried from hunger, been scarred for life by an untreated infection? Only a priest without a cross could say such pretty things about suffering. How could this comfortable lapdog understand that Christ did not come to glorify poverty and suffering but to nail them into his own flesh?

The lapdog was still speaking. "That's why we should think like St. Teresa, who, when faced with the choice between dying and suffering, daily begged and prayed: 'Lord, not death but suffering.' Jesus fled into the street, gasping for air. The sermon was suffocating him. "Christ couldn't have thought like that. Christianity is for men, not slaves. Fighters, not victims." His pain was turning to anger. He almost shouted the words aloud.

Outside, the afternoon was full of people and things, and it was getting cloudy. In front of the church, in a glass case with artificial flowers, was another head of Christ, with red paint for the blood from the thorns. Hands were reaching out to it, hundreds of them, rough hands, beggars' hands. Jesus wanted to clasp every one of these hands, to make these people feel what he was feeling. From inside the church a voice, magnified by microphones, boomed above the sound of the crowd:

Forgive thy people, Lord
Forgive thy people, forgive them, Lord.

Do not be angry forever.
Do not be angry forever.
Forgive them, Lord.

Jesus walked on to get away from the voice. "Forgive them who deceive the people," said the anger in his heart, "the rulers, priests, politicians, businessmen. . . . Forgive everyone who teaches resignation instead of hope. And forgive your people too, for being so everlastingly patient."

II

JUAN SHUT THE BOOK WITH A BANG and thought what did he care about the *tripanosoma gambiensis* or any Latin-named phenomenon whatever. It was stupid and humiliating, to sit meekly, like a slave, cramming one's head with words no one would remember two days after the exam. Worst of all was having to study it from an English book. . . . He stubbed his cigarette out in the ash tray and decided to go and see Jesus. He was bound to be home; he wouldn't have wanted to go to the beach, although Pedro and Andres had tried to persuade him to go with them. "What do I care about *tripanosomas, leishmanias,* kingdoms, classes, families, studies, the university, a professional career? To hell with them all. If I fail, I fail. Better to fail. Then I'll be through with all this garbage. I can kiss it goodbye and go work and live with Jesus." He recalled Jesus' face and felt his heart lift. Just thinking about Jesus made life seem worth living, made all his present preoccupations meaningless and illusory. Jesus seemed to strip life of its familiar baseness, frivolity, and triviality. He lived simply, openhearted toward everyone, befriending everyone. . . .

Juan felt a cheerful warmth go through him. He rose and went to the mirror to comb his hair, dishevelled from too much zoology. The mirror showed him his shining eyes, his youth, and his reddish beard. He felt pleased with his image and smiled and the mirror filled with smile.

"I'm going out," he told his mother.

"Where are you going so early? Tired of studying already?" She came into the room then, small and plump and trying to look stern.

"I'm going for a walk to defog my mind. Zoology bores me silly."

"Bored! Always bored. Everything bores you. If you go on like this you won't pass and you'll lose a year."

Juan shrugged. "I don't care," he said. "What's the point of it all anyway?. . ." "Don't talk like that, Juan. I don't want to hear you saying such things again. After all we've done, your father and I, so that you could be a somebody instead of a nobody, and now you're throwing it all away, just like that. Don't you want to get ahead? Do you want to be a nobody all your life, a poor truck driver like your father?"

Juan smiled and said nothing. He went up to his mother and kissed her forehead.

"Don't worry, old dear. The world isn't entirely divided between somebodies and nobodies. I know what I want, and it's not anything bad."

The kiss made her face relax a little. But then, in place of sternness and reproach, she felt fear. "I don't know," she began, looking Juan in the eyes and choosing her words carefully so as not to annoy him, "but you didn't use to be like this. You say you know what you want now. But you must think of us a bit too. We had such hopes for you, and now. . . . " His mother hesitated. She wished Juan would say something, something to head her away from what she was about to say. But he was silent, and finally she said, "I think that Jesus. . . . " She looked away, and the sentence trailed off, but Juan was already angry.

"There you go again. I've told you not to mention Jesus. I don't know what you've got against him that makes you go on and on about him. If everyone was a bit more like him the world wouldn't be such a shitty place."

His mother tried to mollify him with her eyes. "Don't be like that son," she said in a placating voice. "And there's no need for you to use such language." Juan was furious, but he controlled himself. "It's just that you go over and over it," he said quietly, looking at the floor.

His mother hesitated again. She did not feel reassured, and she was not going to stop giving her son advice even if he did get angry. She took advantage of Juan's lowered eyes. "It's that this Jesus really does frighten me." Another momentary pause for her son's reaction. Then she continued, "I am afraid for you and your brother Santiago. Before you got to know this Jesus, Santiago was much steadier than you, but now even he is all worked up by these ideas that Jesus spouts. I don't know what Jesus does to people. He seems to put a spell on them. No, don't look at me like that! You weren't like this before you met him. You know you weren't! You had ambition, you wanted to get ahead, to be somebody in life. Now all you ever talk about is 'helping others.' You don't care about your studies, you don't care about your future, you don't care about us. I'm not against you wanting to help others, but you must think a bit more about yourself, about your future. . . . " Softly, fearfully, she concluded, ". . . and about us."

She felt defeated. Her son wasn't accepting what she said, but it was hurting him nonetheless. Why this should be so, she did not know; she had intended—she always intended —just the opposite.

Juan didn't know what to say. He made a weary gesture, just to do something. His whole body felt irritable. Then he said: "At any rate, I'm going." The words sounded tired.

"Where—to see him?"

He avoided her eyes.

"I don't know," he said. "I might go over that way."

"Be careful, son, please be careful."

Juan flushed. He began to shout. "All right, all right. Leave me alone. You treat me like a child. I'm fed up with your fussing, your worrying, your nagging. You're always at me. Let me live my own life."

He slammed the door on the way out, but it didn't help. His anger and his mother's voice followed him down the hall together.

"Listen to your mother. She cares about you. They'll fire him again. Everyone says he'll come to a bad end. Think what you're doing, son. Don't wait till it's too late to change."

She was shouting to keep from crying. When the elevator door closed behind him she went to the window and waited for Juan to emerge onto the street below. She simply waited, and after a few moments she saw him come out and walk briskly away in the bright afternoon. "This Jesus," she thought, "I don't know what he's done to my sons. He seems so good, but some people say he's so dangerous. . . . I've got nothing against him, but his ideas are crazy. How can an intelligent boy like him believe that the world will change and be the way he wants?" She looked at the picture of the Nazarene on the wall, crossed herself, and said out loud: "Nazarene of St. Paul, take care of my sons. Don't let anything happen to them, and stop them being friends with Jesus."

III

THE BARRIO LOOKED LIKE A CORPSE, murdered and abandoned. Only the afternoon sun, a pair of eyes at an occasional window, a few people standing wordlessly in doorways. Heat and silence. That was all.

At the door of Jesus' house, he called hello. "Hello, Juancito," said Jesus' mother, opening the door to him. Juan smiled. Her lined, expressive face always made him smile. It had a tranquil, matter-of-fact sweetness that never cloyed. The mere sight of her was refreshing as sweet water.

"Isn't Jesus here?" he asked, still smiling.

"No. He went out just now. He must have gone into town."

The irritable feeling returned with a rush. He was conscious of being tired and sweaty. He made a gesture of impatience.

"But sit down a bit. Don't go yet in this sun. Have some coffee."

Juan sat down and looked at the posters on the walls. He knew them all by heart, but he read them again with interest, as if for the first time. "Justice is not a declaration but a goal." "Love is fighting to make love possible." "In a hungry world no one has the right to waste." "The Christian cannot rest while oppression and injustice exists."

"Here you are, son. Hot coffee is best when you're thirsty."

The fresh coffee smelled good, and he drank it eagerly.

Jesus' mother looked at him, smiling. "How are you doing at school?" he heard her asking.

15

Juan shrugged. "Well," he said, "all right."

"It must be very hard. I don't know how you don't all go mad—having to learn all those things and then remember them. . . ."

"It's not so much that. The worst of it is that most of the things we have to stuff our heads with are completely useless afterwards."

Jesus' mother listened attentively, nodding assent without understanding him. Somehow her incomprehension never irritated him as his own mother's did. It was unfair, he knew, but he couldn't help how he felt, could he? "You have to know so many things these days. . . . Even though Jesus didn't go to college he spends every free minute with his nose in a book. He'd have gone far if he hadn't had to start work so young, after his father died."

"Jesus doesn't need college," said Juan with conviction. "He seems to see the truth of things—wherever he is—clearer than anyone I've ever met."

"Yes," Maria continued, as though Juan had never spoken. She didn't know what Juan meant, though the words were plain enough, but she knew he loved her son, and it made her happy, and the happiness made her reminisce. "Even as a child he wanted to know everything. He asked me the strangest questions—Do trees suffer? Where does the wind sleep? Why do men get drunk and fight? Things like that. Childish things. And I hardly ever knew what to say, so I said just anything. In our village some people said he was a little bit nuts and others said he was very intelligent and we should take him to the city to study. But everyone liked him, even the ones who thought he was strange. He made friends with everybody. He even loved the animals. He used to talk to a little cow we had, as though she were human. And that little cow loved him, you could tell." Abruptly she was quiet. The current of loving reminiscence had carried her unexpectedly against remembered pain, and she sat feeling it again as if for the first time. Finally: "We had to sell the little cow to come here."

Now that she had confessed, as honesty required, what

necessity had made them do, she could finish: "He was never selfish, never! He never even looked out for his own interests. He's been giving away everything he's had ever since he could talk! I can't remember when he didn't care more about other people than about himself."

The reminiscence was over. The selling of the little cow had turned it awry, and though she had managed to conclude she could not continue. Juan felt he should say something— she was waiting for a reply, an acknowledgement of some kind.

"If there were more people like him, the world wouldn't be like it is," he said eventually, and while he said it he was listening to his own words. He had said them often before, they were a formula for something he felt (sometimes he thought they said themselves!), but only now, he thought, did he realize what he meant by them.

Whatever he thought he meant, clearly he had said the right thing. His friend's mother, hearing in the words only praise of her beloved son, was pleased.

"You're a very good boy, too. Try not to turn selfish, like most young men today."

"I'm trying to become more like Jesus," said Juan, and was startled by the tremulousness of his voice.

He said goodbye to Señora Maria and started home. The tranquil pleasure he felt in her company did not redeem the derelict streets or temper the heat. It seemed best to walk without thinking; maybe that way he could preserve the impression of the visit against the surrounding desolation and his own discomfort. A girl waved to him from a doorway. Juan waved back and then began thinking about Lila. He had seen her a few days before, beaten and bruised after a police raid on her school. How could they beat a child so savagely? And such a child, all innocence and gaiety! But she had told him about it as if it were nothing, an adventure, panting out the story like an adorable puppy, while Juan raged inwardly:

"Honestly, that day I hadn't been throwing stones. Other days I did because I like to be part of what's going on, but that day I swear I didn't throw any. I was practicing the piano in the auditorium. All of a sudden old 'Potato-Face' came running and told us to get out—there was going to be a raid on the school. We tried to get out, but there were bullets and stones everywhere. The police were actually throwing stones; I saw them. They threw back the ones the students threw at them. And they were shooting too. When we saw we couldn't get out we went to the cellar under the auditorium, and from there through a window into the dining room. But the women working there chased us out, even though we told them we couldn't go out, we'd be hurt. So we hid in the larder, and the women locked us in. We couldn't breathe in there—there were about twenty of us squashed in with crates of eggs and cans of oil and sacks of rice, so we banged and shouted till they let us out. We went out into the small garden then, till a helicopter flew over it and we hid in the little bath houses out there. I was the only girl there but I hid in this bathhouse for quite a long time with some boys. During a raid, you know, you can't worry about what's proper and what isn't. Then they were banging on the door, and the door opened. 'Out, scum! One by one.' There were three of them, two in civilian clothes and one in uniform. They said: 'Let's leave this one till last. One at a time. Leave me this one till last.' One used his fists, and one had a club, and the last one used the handle of a machete. One of them slugged me from behind as I came out of the bathhouse. 'Faster,' they said, and I hurried as fast as I could but they kept hitting me. It hurt so much I began to cry, and I thought I was going to faint. They took us to the courtyard and made us wait there in the sun for the police van. I saw Ricardo there, all bloody. A man came and flashed a card and said, 'Don't take her. Don't take the blonde girl.' I was scared stiff, and I felt relieved when he said it. Then I heard an officer saying to the men who had hit us, 'Didn't I order you not to touch them?' After that one of the men in civilian clothes came over to me and whispered, 'I hit you with the club, because if I didn't the other man would have hit you with his machete.' And I was supposed to believe that? He wasn't just a pig, he was an idiot too! When the police van came the man who had said not to take me was gone, so they put me inside. One of the soldiers leaned his rifle against me, and I told him to move it because I was really afraid it might go off. I didn't want to get killed, and certainly not by accident. But he just laughed and said, 'You tramp, you wouldn't be much of a loss.' Another cop said to me, 'If you think we're inexperienced, let me tell you, we're not. I've been in uniform three years. You seem to think we're beginners, but you tell me: How long have there been police?' I didn't answer because I didn't know what he was talking about, but he said proudly, 'See! You don't even know. Well let me tell you, there have been police since before Jesus Christ. Did you really not know that? I guess you thought that there were police only for the last few days. Well let me tell you, we're no beginners.' We passed a traffic cop—one of the ones in the caps—and he called out, 'Are you delivering a present?' They yelled back, 'Yes, from Fermin Toro,' and they all laughed. One of the policemen started unloading his rifle, to frighten me I think, and if that's what he wanted, he succeeded. All I could think of was that it would go off. We got to Cotiza exhausted. They let us drink from a filthy tap there, and they made fun of one of the worst hurt students: 'Poor baby, he's hurt.' And they kept poking at his cuts and bruises and repeating, 'Poor thing. How it must hurt! You'll feel better on your knees.' And they made him kneel on the pavement. Then they got to me. They opened my book bag and found some news sheets—the kind that are distributed in schools—which I hadn't even read. 'Look who's carrying communist propaganda. So pretty and a Red. How come? It would serve you right if socialism came. No more fiestas and no more parties, Party-face! You like parties, don't you? Well, if socialism comes there won't be any more. Then you'll know when you were well off. Then you won't even be allowed to paint your nails.' They just kept on like that. But it's not true that socialism means no parties and no painting your fingernails, is it? I'm sure they still paint their nails in Cuba. It was just their dumb way of trying to turn us off socialism. Finally they took away those papers that I hadn't even read. Then they made us sit in twos in the sun.

Then some boys came, they must have been about seventeen years old, wearing police uniforms. One of them said, 'You can go in the shade.' And he came with me and began talking to me. 'Do you know what plant this is?' I didn't. 'Potato,' he told me. I didn't say anything. 'Come on, you don't fool me. It's marijuana, and you know it.' I don't know if he was telling the truth because I don't know what potato plants or marijuana plants look like. Then they called us into the police station one by one. We were booked and photographed. They said I was a 'disseminator of subversive literature.' Then they asked me if I'd like some coffee with milk. I was grateful and said yes because I was actually very hungry, but suddenly I was dizzy too and didn't know if I could hold anything down. I needn't have worried, though, because they didn't give me any coffee. They made some and drank it themselves in front of me and laughed at me. One of them gave a dumb, dirty laugh and said, 'If you want some, baby, I can give you milk—but without coffee.' They all thought that was wildly funny; a couple more made the same offer. At about six in the evening they lined us up at attention and told us they were going to give us back our I.D. cards and papers. A major or somebody said that he knew which of us had previously been involved in robberies or antigovernment rioting. Just like that—as if an angel had come to him with the information! He also said that anyone without an I.D. card obviously wasn't a student but an outside agitator—and we all knew what happened to 'outside agitators,' didn't we? I knew the kids who didn't have their cards with them; they all attended my school and some of them were in my classes. It seemed pointless to say to these goons that it's easy to lose an I.D. card when you're being arrested and beaten up. They must have lost their cards. People had been waiting for us outside since two o'clock. Then the Chief showed up and made us a speech. He assured us he had a degree in science and a degree in humanities and one in law and God knows how many other degrees in other subjects, and that when he was young he too had had revolutionary ideas but that he had understood in good time that nothing could be achieved by riots and rock throwing. It was true that we had problems, but he was there for us to bring them to. And finally he got to his real point, which was that if they had to raid the school again they'd really cream us. 'We'll use other measures,' he said. 'We won't be as gentle as we were today.' When he'd gotten his message across, an absolutely gorgeous major, with green eyes, spoke to us. He said he agreed with everything the Chief said, and that we should cooperate and do our duty, as Bolivar would want, and that we should be like him. I looked at him the whole time because, although he was talking garbage, he looked stupendous, particularly those eyes. Then the speeches were over, and we were dismissed in groups of five. I was in the last group. My parents were waiting for me outside and they got all excited when they saw the state I was in. As usual, my father got mad and lectured and my mother was terrified and didn't say a word. 'Look what happens when you get mixed up in things that are none of your business. I hope you've finally learned your lesson.' My mother just hugged me. Finally my father was finished bawling me out, and they took me to a cafe because it was very late and I hadn't had anything to eat all day."

Juan remembered that when she finished her story Lila had asked him for a cigarette. Silent, and puffing with some difficulty at her cigarette, she looked even prettier. Juan smiled, then he shook his head to clear away the memory. He saw a bus coming and caught it without stopping to think.

IV

WHAT WAS HE DOING ON THE BUS? Going downtown to look for Jesus, that's what, going to look for one man who might be in downtown Caracas on Wednesday in Holy Week! A fool's errand, if ever there was a fool and his errand, but he needed to find Jesus. He needed to be with him, talk to him, listen to him. Especially listen. His common sense chattered like a monkey about wasted time and bus fare, but his need was carrying him downtown as surely as the bus, if less perceptibly.

The bus was half empty and so was the road, and the speed of the bus sent a pleasant breeze through the open windows. Juan felt his hot face cool. He closed his eyes.

He had first heard of Jesus from a newspaper article about a hunger strike outside the INOS offices by ten workers demanding water for their district. The article named one Jesus Rodriguez, resident in Gramoven, as the strike leader. The press paid little attention to the strike but five days later he read an interview in *Punto* in which Jesus said that they were striking because it was the only way to bring their demands to public attention, as they had already tried every other means and none had worked, and they had no water to wash with and so scabies had broken out, and when they got water they had to pay four bolivars a keg for it, sometimes more. He went on to call it preposterous and inhuman that Venezuela, super-rich from its oil, should be sick with all the symptoms of poverty: slums and unemployment and illiterate, illegitimate, starving people. The government, he said, was prepared to spend millions on its "image," offering Caracas as host city for the upcoming international conference on uses of the sea; for a lot less money it could fix itself up, by giving them their water and helping poor people find a way out of their poverty. He concluded by saying that there they were and there they would stay till the end, "motivated by their principles as human beings, Venezuelans, and Christians." Juan was astonished, chiefly by that last word in the mouth of a workingman that the press routinely described as a hothead, an agitator, and a pro-Marxist.

That very day he had sought Jesus out. He had found him surrounded by people, some obviously curiosity-seekers, the rest, who were watching him gravely, neighbors. He was dark, about thirty, slight but strong, with sunstreaked hair and a broad forehead. Juan had stayed near him for a little while, looking at him without daring to say anything. He had hoped Jesus would open his eyes and look at him, but he didn't. He was probably very weak from fasting and seemed to be asleep. Beside him were two women, an older one who must have been his mother and a younger one, still beautiful, who looked as if she had been crying and who Juan thought must be his wife. Juan had hung around, considering whether to speak to them, but his shyness prevented him and finally he went home, reproaching himself for his reticence.

A few days later he had read that INOS had agreed to install the water supply on condition that the people of the district dig the drains for the pipes. He hurried over to see and found work already begun. The whole project seemed quite informally organized, but it looked to be going forward smoothly. People were putting their backs into it, but cheerfully, making small jokes as they worked. Juan felt awkward and out of place but unable to leave. He went and stood as close as possible to where Jesus was working, and watched him.

"Give us a hand, baby, we don't need sidewalk superintendents," called a woman who was digging beside Jesus.

Juan recognized her. She was the younger of the two who had been with Jesus during the hunger strike.

"He's not the working kind, Madalena," said a very thin girl with a flowered kerchief on her head. "Can't you see he's got the hands of a little gentleman?"

Jesus stopped digging a moment to wipe his face. He looked straight at Juan and smiled.

"He looks strong," he said and beckoned to Juan to join them.

Juan felt absurdly happy. He leaped into the ditch.

"Let me," he said, grabbing the pick from the woman working next to Jesus. The handle was wet with sweat.

"It's hard work if you're not used to it," said the woman, smiling. "Tell me when you start getting blisters."

Juan fell to work with enthusiasm. The earth was hard and the pick bounced in his inexperienced hands, but he felt joyful.

"So the little gentleman can work after all?" said the girl with the flowered kerchief.

"And he's handsome too," said Madalena by way of reply.

Juan grinned, his face red with embarrassment and exertion. He was trying to time the strokes of his pick to Jesus' firm, regular ones. Within moments his vest was soaked with sweat. Then Jesus leaned on his pick and turned to look at him. Juan went on working for a bit, pretending not to notice. Then he too stopped, and smiled at Jesus. He had the uncanny feeling that Jesus knew his thoughts, that Jesus understood him much better than he understood himself.

"Where are you from?" asked Jesus.

"Avenida Sucre, in Catia."

"What's your job?"

"I don't work. I study. I'm in my first year at the university."

Jesus only nodded. Juan lowered his eyes and began kicking a lump of earth.

"Why did you come here?" he heard Jesus' voice over his shoulder.

He looked up again. Jesus was smiling at him, inviting him to be friends.

"I wanted to see if I could help, that's all," he said. And then, stroking the pick handle: "I wanted to talk to you, too."

"To me? How do you know me?"

"I've been wanting to talk to you for some time," said Juan. "I saw you during your hunger strike. I was watching you one day when you didn't see me. . . ."

The streets were filled with cars, people, sidewalk vendors, voices. He saw a beggar with no legs and children dressed in purple, he heard a confused noise and smelled incense.

Juan began to walk toward St. Teresa's. The sidewalk vendors were offering Sacred Hearts, icons, saints' medals, crosses, bottles, incense, seeds, prayer cards for all occasions. In front of St. Teresa's was a huge crowd trying to jam its way inside. The vendors slid sideways through the crowd, offering their wares. Juan moved toward the church amid a tumult of voices. Hollow voices, as if they came from hungry bellies.

"Picture and prayer of the Nazarene of St. Paul. Picture and prayer of the Nazarene of St. Paul."

"The mighty Nazarene of St. Paul."

"One bolivar, one bolivar. Picture and prayer of the Nazarene."

A little girl was eating a chocolate bar. Eyes, many eyes, painted blue and green.

"The Lady, she'll drive away enemies. The Lady, she'll keep wicked enemies away from your house."

"Take the Lady. The Lady. She'll drive away wicked enemies. Only one bolivar. The Lady."

"The Lady. The Mighty Hand."

Some very young firemen were carrying from the church a small girl who had fainted. They left her at the first-aid station in the square and ran back, eager to be seen and admired.

"Three candles for a bolivar. Three candles for a bolivar."

"Incense sticks. Incense. The Lady. One bolivar each, one bolivar."

People were milling about in front of the statue of Christ in the church doorway. It was covered with old dust and badly faded by the sun.

"A medal for a bolivar."

A skinny, dry, dark-skinned hand shoved a lottery ticket in Juan's face.

"They haven't got a barbecue here, have they?" asked a woman who smelled pleasantly of perfume.

A cripple was counting five-bolivar notes in a corner. Juan didn't see Jesus in the crowd, but there was no chance to look for him now. He was at the church door and the crowd pushed him inside.

There was a huge pile of candles just to the left of the doorway, but a policeman stood over them, repeating, "No lit candles in the church."

"It's because of the fire that year," Juan heard a very stout woman saying.

Inside, the priest's sanctimonious drone dominated all other sounds. It made him sick to his stomach, as always:

"Because our Nazarene is a hundred percent Venezuelan, made of Venezuelan material, carved of Venezuelan wood by a Venezuelan artist, because our Christ is a Creole Christ, not foreign or imported, that's why he understands us and loves us. And you love our Venezuelan Nazarene too, don't you?"

"Yes," came the roar from the close-packed bodies around Juan.

"You are proud to be Christians and followers of our Venezuelan Christ, aren't you?"

"Yes," came the roar again, even louder than before.

The priest was working the crowd into a frenzy—and apparently himself along with it. He was ranting now. Juan could not see him, but the hysterical voice conjured up a red face and popping eyes.

"You are prepared to defend your Creole Nazarene against all the church's enemies, aren't you?"

This time the "yes" was hysterical. Juan saw two men make their way out, shaking their heads. He looked at them and gave a barely perceptible nod. Whatever they were thinking, he probably agreed, and he wanted them to know it. He craved the presence of a kindred spirit, the assurance that somewhere in the mindless crowd another mind was resisting the priest's crude propaganda.

The priest's voice was cracking now:

"We do not want fanaticism! We are not fanatics! But we Venezuelans defend our religion because we defend our Nazarene. Do we want the enemies of Christ to triumph in our country?"

"Noooo!"

Juan began pushing his way out. If he didn't get away from that voice, he thought, he would hit someone or break something out of helpless rage. Besides, Jesus couldn't possibly be in here, and he needed to see Jesus. When he emerged onto the street the bells were pealing, not "making a joyful noise unto the Lord" but tolling sorrow or doom. The sky was darkening. A child squealed for joy, a separate, different sound clearly audible at close range against the clangor of the bells. Then the bells stopped, and the sidewalk vendors began again to cry their wares.

"Incense sticks for one bolivar with the prayer of the Nazarene. One bolivar. Yours for one bolivar."

"Incense sticks for one bolivar. Camomile for one bolivar."

"Powerful Prayer of the Lonely Soul. Incense sticks, Camomile, one bolivar, one bolivar."

"Prayer for the Spirit of Abandonment."

"Prayer for the Unquiet Soul."

"Incense sticks, stations of the cross, the Prayer of Tobacco."

"The Don Juan of Money. Prayer to the Stone of Zamuro."

Juan felt assaulted and overwhelmed by the voices. His eyes lit on a black man, nearly bald, with an enormous compensatory moustache. He was shouting in a thick, greasy voice.

"What is this man thinking as he shouts? Who is his God? Who is the God of our people?"

Juan walked on. He noticed a pair of trousers stretched over a fat behind, with a heart appliquéd on each side so as to jiggle at every step. A man with a thick neck. He crossed the street and up a flight of steps crawling with vendors. Diego Ibarra Square was full of people. Children were crossing and recrossing the square, doing nothing, killing time. Knots of soldiers, in uniform, pimply, were eyeing the girls. Neon-lit fountains made mountain-water sounds amid the sounds of the city. A white half-moon, barely visible in the yellowish sky.

Juan looked for a quiet place to sit down. He needed to order his impressions and feelings and thoughts. Suddenly there was Jesus, sitting down, watching some children, and looking happy. Instantly Juan felt his heart lighten and grow calm.

"Hello," he said and sat down beside him.

"Hello, Juan." How, Juan wondered, could a common-place greeting and a smile make a person feel as if he'd just received a precious gift?

"I was just walking this way," he said diffidently, suddenly unwilling to have Jesus know he had been looking for him. "I was in St. Teresa's for a little while, till I couldn't stand it any longer. It seemed to be a revival meeting. The priest was whipping up the people to acclaim the Nazarene, calling him a hundred percent Venezuelan Christ made of Creole materials by a Creole artist. You should have heard him!" In spite of himself, Juan was smiling.

"I was there too," said Jesus. "I saw our people idolizing the Nazarene. And I heard that sermon whose every word embodied religion as the opiate of the people. Marx would have been delighted, but I had to leave. That sermon made me nauseous.

Juan got out his cigarettes, and they smoked in silence for a while. "You thought it was sickening," said Juan presently, "and I thought it was sickening. And I saw two other people walk out in the middle. But everyone else thought it was great, and everyone else was an awful lot of people."

"The people's faith is confused but deep," said Jesus. "They believe firmly, fervently. They need to believe."

"But their faith doesn't help their liberation, it hinders it," said Juan. "Why don't they see that? What do they really believe about God?"

Jesus said nothing. A very pale girl with a scarred face went by. Twilight was falling on the square, and the cupolas of St. Teresa's were darkening against the orange sky. The fountains spouted colored water, and from somewhere soft music began, mingling with the noise and the voices. "Our people are able to believe," said Jesus, looking at the late afternoon light, "in an imprecise, mixed-up way. They believe in God and in all the saints without much distinction. And they believe in brotherhood with everyone else who is poor. Their faith is an actual sharing, a continual giving. But they don't philosophize about it much, so if the priests tell them, in their best churchy voices, that faith means bringing offerings of fruit to church, they'd accept that. In Latin America liberation will become inevitable when Christians understand their faith as a political struggle for a just society, in which there are no exploiters or exploited, but only brothers and sisters."

"Didn't Che Guevara say something like that?"

"Whether he did or not, this must be the heart of Christianity, or any religion based on love. Real love can't tolerate injustice. The fact that Christianity, whose very foundation is love, has survived in an unjust society just means that it has been totally distorted. But it still has the power, among the people, to return to its truth."

Again they were silent. A plane roared overhead, an old woman in brightly colored slacks went by, and a girl paraded up and down. Night came down from the hill and the colored jets of water shone more brightly in the dark. The people stayed on, strolling and chatting, enjoying their feast-day leisure to the full.

Jesus looked up at the sky. "Look, a star is out," and he pointed. Juan looked up and then down again to the brightly lit towers opposite. He looked at sailors hopefully following girls, at photographers slung with cameras, at mothers chatting as their children played, at people sitting around the fountain, at the buildings, and at the bright night, which contained all but hid nothing. He wished he could put a name to how he felt, but his state of mind was like nothing he'd ever experienced before: happy nervousness, fearful exultation, reluctant anticipation, God knows what, except that it was many feelings all mixed up together. Jesus, his new acquaintance, was simply sitting next to him; Jesus, the cause of his agitation, was a ferment in his mind; Jesus, who so matter-of-factly observed that Christianity was earthly justice or it was nothing, seemed remote as the stars. The silence was making him nervous, and he fidgeted on the concrete bench, trying to find words.

"I heard you got fired again," he said with an effort.

Jesus, who had been lost in thought, returned his attention to Juan.

"Yes," he said, as matter-of-factly as he had spoken of love and justice. "Yesterday they gave me my pay and told me they no longer required my services."

Juan's eyes showed more pain than Jesus'.

"Did they give reasons?" he asked angrily.

Jesus smiled. "The usual pretexts. They must have found out that we were planning to form a union."

Juan felt himself trembling with anger. Injustice was horrible, but that injustice should victimize his hero was insupportable. "Stinking, lousy, rotten sons-of-bitches!" he said through clenched teeth. "What are you going to do?"

Jesus shrugged. "The usual. Start again. Look for work again. Try to unionize again, wherever I find work."

"Don't you ever get tired of having to start again?"

Jesus looked at him. His voice remained level, but his eyes were burning. "Of course I get tired. But final victory is ours. Knowing that, I never lose hope, and hope gives strength."

"How are you so sure?" asked Juan very low.

Jesus did not reply for a moment.

"From my faith in the people"—he paused for a moment and then went on—"and my faith in God, which is the same faith." His normally unemphatic voice was deeper than Juan had ever heard it, as if the words had been a solemn promise.

They got up then and began to walk toward the bus stop. In

the deepening dark the soldiers' uniforms were becoming invisible but the sailors' uniforms looked even whiter. They left the square. Caracas smelled of cars, beer, incense, and grilled meat. They walked past St. Francis' Church. A young nun with a remote, dreamy expression was selling scapulars and little icons. Peddlers hawked prayer cards, offering remedies for all pains and sicknesses.

"Saints and prayers for every need!" cried one. He was all dark—hair, skin, eyes. Only his moustache was white.

"Oh what a lovely little saint. How much?" asked a woman longingly.

There were so many people. All ages and classes, but mostly poor. The people. Believing. Wanting to believe.

V

JUDAS THOUGHT HE MUST BE GOING MAD WITH DOUBT. His food and drink were tasteless with doubt; the air he breathed was doubt, and it choked him. His doubt infested him like cancer, becoming flesh of his flesh, will of his will—becoming Judas Martinez.

He flung out of his room, not hearing the door slam behind him, and wandered streets whose names he did not know, among people and cars he did not see, trampling the afternoon underfoot.

When night came, he was at the rectory asking for Father Sanchez.

"He's not here at the moment. He must be in church hearing confessions," answered a woman's voice after an interminable wait.

Judas ran to the church. Doubt running, pursued by doubt as by the furies.

Long queues were waiting in front of the confessionals; the people stood patiently but looked nervous from the long wait. Judas looked at his watch. The light was dim and he held it up to see the numbers, but though he saw the numbers clear enough now, he could not tell what time they told. He wiped his forehead and shivered with anxiety.

He went out into the lamp-lit, almost starless night and found himself sitting on a bench. A breeze stirred his hair. Who was this Jesus? Why couldn't he stop thinking about him? Why did he hate him so? Or did he really love him? How could anyone tell what they really felt? Who, really, was this Jesus? Answer after answer crashed through his brain like breakers: a guerrilla, a saint, a ne'er-do-well, a rebel, a good man, a communist, a sage—his bewilderment and uncertainty were unbearable. He shook his head again, painfully, but the shaking failed to clear it. It didn't even distract him from his pain. What ought he to do? He, Judas, had gone to Father Sanchez's meetings and had sworn to be faithful to Christ. Since then he had lived his faith whole-heartedly, untroubled and happy. At the meetings people testified fervently to their faith in Christ and bolstered each others' religious enthusiasm. They came out of those meet-ings glowing with Christian commitment against a world that despised the faith. But then he had met Jesus, and a breach had opened in his faith, and in it doubts had grown. At first they were insignificant, but the more he talked to Jesus the stronger they became. Now they had taken over his whole self and were killing him.

Judas owned a grocery store, and one day he had refused a woman credit. It was only common sense. She was an old customer, but she was out of work, had no money, and giving her more credit was just giving the food away. It wasn't his fault, but the woman went off crying, and her flock of kids began crying too when they saw their mother cry. Later—an hour, maybe—the shop door opened, and that was the first time he ever laid eyes on Jesus.

"Shopkeeper! Thief! Making money off people's hunger! You fatten on your people's corpses! Give me the bolivar's worth of bread you refused that woman, and a pound of rice, some oil, and a canned ham with it."

Judas wanted to throw this insolent s.o.b. out of his store, but a second look made him hesitate. He wasn't very big, this person, but something in his expression gave one pause. Besides, Caruao's two brothers, looking grim, were ranged behind him.

"I'm no thief," he said, prudently choosing argument over force. "I fight for justice."

The man's face became even more terrifyingly stern.

"You call it justice to have a full store and refuse a bit of bread to a starving woman and children? You call it justice to pay your clerks a miserable seven bolivars a day just because they have to take it—because any job is better than no job?"

"Seven bolivars is better than nothing," shrugged Judas. He glanced at Jesus to gauge the effect of his words. "And I help them out with food. Maybe it's not a king's ransom, but it's better than starving."

It was, Judas thought, a reasonable answer, not cowardly but not provocative either. Why, then, was Jesus thundering at him with blazing eyes?

"People like you, people without mercy, should be in prison where they couldn't exploit anyone! Yes, Judas, your true place is behind bars!"

"Is this going to be when Venezuela goes communist?" The best defense, after all, is to counter-attack, and what better counter-attack than to call the man a communist?

Jesus shook his head. He didn't look angry anymore, only sad, but he still spoke sternly: "No, it will be when Venezuela goes genuinely Christian," he said, pointing at the pink Christ Judas had put up over the cash register.

Feeling safer now, Judas permitted himself a sarcastic reply. "Who are you to come in here like this and give me lessons in Christianity? What seminary did you study theology in? Or was it at a university?"

Jesus paused. The anger seemed to leave him, and his voice, when he answered, was astonishingly gentle. "Do you think you have to go to school to understand that Christianity means love?"

Who the hell was this man who was impervious to sweet reason, to the imputation of being a Red, to personal jibes? Why did he, Judas, feel like an accused criminal under that look? "I do love," he said. "I help them as much as I can."

"But you love your money more, don't you, Judas?"

You couldn't even shout at a man speaking so low and calmly!

"I've got the right to get ahead," said Judas, not looking up. "It's not up to me to solve all the world's problems."

"Nobody is asking you to solve all the world's problems. I'm only asking you not to exploit your neighbors and get rich on their hunger."

It was an extraordinary first meeting, and even more extraordinary that they sought each other out quite often afterward. They had long, calm conversations. They became, in the end, close friends. Judas became enthusiastic about Jesus' ideas and began to take an active part in the committee for improving the neighborhood. They had installed drains, gotten piped-in water, built a school. . . . Certainly the neighborhood was being transformed by Jesus' ideas and example. But wasn't he going too far? Now he was talking about creating a powerful organization to change Venezuela. He said we were living in an inhuman world that had to be destroyed to create a new one. Wasn't this communism? Yes, this Jesus was clever enough to act devout in order to deceive the people and manipulate them. But what he said wasn't Christian. He attacked private property, condemned the rich, called politicians demagogues and priests businessmen. . . . His picture of a real Christian was actually a communist; he said that Christian faith must be expressed in revolutionary actions, even against religion itself when it supported an unjust world.

Christianity . . . communism . . . humanity . . . revolution . . . Judas decided to take his questions and his doubts to Father Sanchez. But the priest had exasperated rather than calmed his perturbation. "Be careful of that man." Father Sanchez's eyes and voice were anxious. "Don't trust wolves in sheep's clothing, don't trust false prophets. The Church alone holds the truth. She is the only true guide. Think where you are headed, Judas. Aren't you breaking your promise to be faithful to Christ? Does this man go to Mass on Sunday? Does he take the sacraments? Does he defend the Church's interests? Haven't you told me he even attacks them? How can God be in him if he is in mortal sin? Judas, be careful. You are being tempted by the enemy. Keep away from that man, he has the devil in him. And don't forget that social problems aren't everything. Christ himself said that in this world the poor would be always with us."

Judas had left feeling worse than when he came. Nothing was resolved. Inside his head, Father Sanchez's words and Jesus' clashed. In this frame of mind, headed for home, he had run into Jesus.

"Hello, Judas, where to?"

"Just coming back from a walk," he said, looking down.

"You look worried. Something happen?"

Judas looked up and shook his head, but his face was an open book and denied his denial.

"Something's very wrong, I can see. Can I help?"

Judas winced perceptibly.

"Tell me the truth," he said. "Who are you? What do you want around here?"

Jesus smiled. "You know what I want, Judas. The same as you. That one day we can all live like brothers and sisters. That each day we make the world a bit better."

The reply only aggravated his distress.

"You're a Communist!" He himself could not have told whether he was hurling a denunciation or asking a question. He had said it as an accusation, so why was he waiting for an answer?

Jesus laid his hand on Judas' shoulder, but Judas jerked nervously away.

"Don't worry about words, Judas," said Jesus. "Don't try to pigeonhole people in categories you've learned from other people. I want my brothers' and sisters' well-being. I believe in my brothers and sisters and I love them. And I believe in God and love him. God gives me strength." He waited a moment for the noise of a passing motorbike to recede. "Don't judge people by what they say but by what they do. And be at peace. That's where God is—in peace, not in worry. But you live in a state of worry. . . ."

"It's because I don't know who or what to believe. I started to worry when I met you. Before that everything was so uncomplicated. I was secure and happy in my life and in my faith."

Jesus said nothing, so Judas pressed on: "Don't you think you are going too far?"

"Judas, do you call it going too far when there is so much poverty and squalor around us, when 'look out for Number One' is the first law of life for most people? Don't you think that, on the contrary, we haven't yet begun?"

"Christ himself said that there will always be the poor in the world," said Judas firmly, girding himself with Father Sanchez's argument.

"Maybe he did. But he didn't mean that this is the way things ought to be. Yes, there will always be poor people. Some people are poor because they have nothing, and some are poor because whatever they have they want more. They're the poor rich—they don't want to share, they're terrified that what belongs to everyone will be taken away from them. Just because there will always be the poor, our lives must always be a struggle against poverty."

"There's no use talking to you," cried Judas. "You twist everything."

"Isn't it rather your doubts that keep twisting what is simple and clear?"

Judas had no answer. He turned abruptly and went away, still harboring the pain of all his doubts.

VI

CRAZY MARRERO OPENED HIS FRONT DOOR and went out into the dark. He told whoever was listening that he had been a seminarian and all that studying had driven him mad, and that some nights he was possessed by spirits. On those nights he went outside and preached, long and loudly and sorrowfully. Tonight his eyes shone like diamonds. He seemed moon-struck, and indeed a crescent moon hung in the sky. He looked blindly at the houses poking everywhere out of the ground and went tirelessly and soundlessly to the top of the hill. Standing there in the dark, he hurled his words against the sleeping houses.

"They speak of justice and rights. They are just words. They do not speak from the heart, only from the mouth. They speak of justice and their minds are on the cut they are going to take for themselves. They think of justice as a sharing out of the crumbs left over from their own meal. And we are satisfied with the crumbs, we fight over them. In our eagerness to devour them we devour one another. We are not united. That's why we believe them when they talk about justice and we look up like dogs to see where their leavings are going to fall. Listen, all of you! I know you can hear me in the night. We are not united, and that is why we believe their words."

Crazy Marrero wrapped his arms around his thin shoulders and stood silently on the dark hilltop. It seemed he would say no more, when suddenly he raised his voice again and shouted:

"They are robbing us of ourselves. We are a people who are not a people. We are voiceless. We belong to others. Yankee Venezuela, fucked by all comers. Where are our Venezuelans? They have sucked us dry; we are all nothings. We rant about Revolution and Patriotism and it's nothing but noise. Revolution—Patriotism—People—noise from mouths stinking of whiskey and mouthwash. Blasphemers! Liars! Yankee-hearted Venezuelans!"

The madman's voice pelted the neighborhood like heavy rain. No one thought to tell him to be quiet. "Crazy Marrero is at it again. He's not going to let us sleep. He'll be preaching at us all night," they whispered, and they began to listen.

Crazy Marrero raised his voice a third time. Now he sounded as if he were lecturing to students sitting in a circle around him in the night.

"We have all seen how ants work. They are tiny but they work together, and together they can move mountains. But we, we work—every one of us—for himself, exploiting others if we can. We are not united. We look down on ants, but we are less than ants; they accomplish what we cannot. Now you'll say: These are the ravings of Crazy Marrero. But pay attention to my words. They are full of sense. The good listener does not need many words, but there is no listener worse than one who does not want to hear. We are turning into a flock of sheep driven by foreign propaganda. We are a pack of imitators—monkey-see-monkey-do, is all we're good for. We've lost ourselves. What is Venezuela? Oil, highways, ranches, discotheques, pop music, big cars, and beauty contests. Peasants dying of hunger, and women who sell themselves in the street to live. Venezuela, land of murderers. How long must we endure all these murderers on television, on the radio, in congress, and in the classrooms. Murderers with make-up and white hands. Murderers who bleed us and sell our blood to foreigners. Is there no one who will speak out against these murderers? Venezuela, you are no longer Venezuela, you don't exist, they won't let you exist. They want to make you into a continental Puerto Rico, and they are succeeding. I curse the oil that is drowning us! I curse the oilmen who have bled us dry for their oil, who have traded their own blood for cologne flowing in their veins. Traitors who talk nationalism and go and rest from their speechifying in Miami or New York. Venezuela is dying. It has been sold to the highest bidder. It has been sucked dry by vampires."

Again he was silent for a long time. When he resumed it was in a softer, almost pleading tone:

"Yes, Venezuela is lost, but we are going to recover it. We will ordain justice and bring it to life. We will not wait for others to do it for us. We are going to establish justice in this country. By our work and by our unity. It will be a reality, not just a word. A powerful reality. We must be united, as Jesus says. He is my friend, Jesus Rodriguez, and he is a good man and we should listen to him. We must unite, because divided we can achieve nothing. And we must all work. We have no place for young, able-bodied people who pass their days hand in hand endlessly listening to Yankee music. No more. Everyone who can must work. Those who won't work had better lie low or we'll make them work. Brothers, it is not right that there should be so many idlers when there is so much to struggle for. It is not right. We are going to change things. Venezuela is going to become Venezuelan again. We will work to make it so. But all together, like ants moving mountains. You remember? Give me your hand and let me work with you. Take my hand, I'll go where you lead me. That's what each of us must say. That's how we must work. Not like our leaders, who get rich by their own uselessness. All they are are examples of what not to be. We are better than they."

Again he paused for a long time. You could hear the night sounds. Far off a dog barked, roused by the sound of his voice.

"And this is not communism, as the traitors say," Crazy Marrero continued. "No, do not misunderstand me. This is not communism, because I am a good Christian. I believe in God, Mary, and the saints. People who say there is no God are wrong. They are mad, not I. They say there is no God, and they tremble at the very thought of death. They say there is no God, and this makes it easier for them to neglect people. That's why their justice is a false, meaningless word. They are mad, not I. I believe in God, Mary, and the saints. I am not ashamed to say so. That's why I am sure that this is not communism. Communism is something quite different. Very few people know what communism really is. Even I don't know very well, but I know that what I'm saying is not communism. Working together to bring justice is not communism. Communism's got nothing to do with it. Ants are not communists, because they worked like that before communism was invented. Can ants be communists? Have any of you heard of any country, however capitalist, where they imprison and persecute ants for being communists? That's why I'm telling you that when I say we are going to work together, that isn't communism. That's how we'll make Venezuela great, by God, as it is already. Greatness is not money or oil, or iron, or gold. Only people can be great. And if the leaders are corrupt and useless, we shall be the great ones to make Venezuela great. We can do it if we cooperate, if we really get to work.

"And what I'm saying isn't what Hitler said either. You know what Hitler did. That is not the way to greatness. We will not invade other countries or enslave people or murder Jews. Jews who hear me, have no fear! And the Colombians don't have to be afraid either, because we are not going to invade them. We are not going to do what Hitler did. I am no Nazi or fascist. I am a Venezuelan who wants to make his country great by the work of its people. No more drugs, no more idleness, no envy and no imported vices. And no self-pitying sentimentality, either. I know of two young men around here going around with long beards and long hair and long faces—no use to anyone, even themselves. And why for Christ's sake? Because a woman rejected them! Must the world come to an end for that? No swooning Romeos! And no drug dealers. I'll be on the lookout for them. I'll be like a public health officer with a thousand eyes, and when I see filth I'll go straight to the authorities. Straight to the authorities. Because we should not be afraid of the authorities, we should respect them. If they stop you, stand still. Don't run away. Better to lose a minute of your life than to lose your life in a minute. Listen well, all of you: If they stop you, stand still, don't run. Only criminals need to run away. Going to prison isn't the worst thing. A week, two weeks, a month in prison is better than losing your life. Life is sweet even when it seems bitter."

The madman stopped again, with his last sentence lingering in the silence. He fingered his matted beard and stared into the darkness. And once again words came flooding out of him:

"This is Holy Week, and all people think about is going to the beach and having fun. You don't make your country great by going to the beach. We call it Holy Week and we turn it into a week of sin. Pleasure and diversion absorb us, and we don't notice—on the beach—that our country is bleeding to death, that we are all bleeding to death. The ones who aren't at the beach are watching the processions. They cry over the painted wounds on the wooden saints and never notice the real wounds in the flesh of their brothers and sisters beside them. So Holy Week becomes a week of sin. We worship pleasure or we worship idols, and either way we don't notice God dying right next to us in the crowd. And who are his executioners? We are! We damn the Romans and persecute the Jews, but they didn't kill him—we are killing him! We who keep crucifying each other! We lie on the beach and we cry over wooden saints and we devour each other while God dies among us. And we call it Holy Week."

"Shut up, crackpot, shut up and let us sleep!" A child screamed.

"I can't shut up. I must say what must be said."

"Shut up, you're cracked, now shut up," cried the child again.

Crazy Marrero looked around as if seeking the voice.

"Ricardo, I recognize your voice. If I don't speak I feel I'll die tonight."

"Well, die then, loony, and leave us alone to get some sleep."

"Listen, child, you shouldn't talk like that to a grown-up. They call me mad, but I've supported myself all my life, and I have children who have children. I'm an honest man and an honest worker, and I've never harmed a soul. With my own hands I supported my family. Now my children have children. Your people don't teach you respect, child, and if I gave you the spanking you deserve they'd be at me like animals for hitting 'one of theirs.' Why don't they care what's right instead of what's theirs? Why do they let you make fun of me? God commands me to speak. Why should I be mocked?"

The madman ceased, and there was no answer. The whole neighborhood was silent. Marrero lay on the ground looking at the stars and thought it would be good to die. He began to feel sleepy.

MAUNDY THURSDAY

VII

In caruao outside the bar called negro primero, Pedro, Andres, and Tomas were lying on the sand drinking beer. The sea was green on the surface, azure if you looked into its depths. The waves rose lazily and broke monotonously against the beach. The sun baked the sand and glittered on the water. There were several small groups of people on the beach, orange and blue tents, and farther away near the river mouth a larger crowd of bodies and voices.

Pedro took a long swallow of beer. He wiped his mouth with his forearm and belched. "Beer gets warm so fast," he said. Nobody answered.

From the bar behind him the juke box belted out for the thousandth time:

> Came wind and flood and hit me,
> A light I had that lit me. . . .

Pedro swore between his teeth and thought about going in to change the record and order more beer. But he didn't. He stretched his legs on the warm sand and looked at the haze rising off the sea.

Gradually the beach began to fill up. A group of young people trekked in, dusty and sweaty and weighed down by knapsacks. Pedro smiled, silently playing detective: To get away from the crowds, they had walked all the way from Los Caracas, along the hilly and dusty road through Osma, Oritapo, Todasana, and La Sabana; they were proud of having come so far under their own steam, and they wanted to be noticed for it. They wore their knapsacks jauntily, like badges of honor.

"Good kids, those," said a woman's voice, "walking from Los Caracas in all this heat."

"You're right, they're from Caracas, from the school of Jesus the Worker," replied another woman. "It's a long walk on a hot day."

Pedro remembered how empty the beach was when he was a child. No Negro Primero Bar, no dirt road, only a few fishermen's huts. The fishermen were dark and healthy, like himself. Early mornings they put out to sea, returning in mid-afternoons to laze in their doorways, chatting and slapping away the mosquitoes while the women gutted and smoked the catch. The old men spun endless tales about Mandinga and the English who put out his yellow skeleton on windy nights. For St. John's Day and the May festival there were drums, and they all danced till they dropped, dizzy with the rhythm and the rum that had been brought by sea from La Guaira.

One day when he was about twelve his father had taken him and his brother Andres to Caracas. They were abashed and dismayed by the big city. The cars, the buildings, the shops, the clothes, the city women dazzled Pedro's senses and aroused in him a profound feeling of his own inferiority and an indomitable ambition to return to Caracas and become a success there when he was older. At sea in his father's fishing boat Pedro dreamed of the city and imagined himself as one of the heroes he had seen in the movies in La Guaira, worshipped by white-skinned women who swooned into his arms with love. He had fantasies of amazing exploits and adventures, and while his eyes searched the sea for fish he pictured himself as an ace detective, a demon motorcyclist, a tycoon with a Cadillac and a vast and gleaming wardrobe.

"Pedro, you rowing or sleeping?" called his father.

"He's daydreaming."

The others laughed.

"He must be in love," said his brother Andres maliciously.

Then Pedro rowed with all his might, feeling the perfect

rhythmic rippling of his muscles, feeling his own strength, feeling the boat respond ("like a woman," he thought) to the strength of his arms. He rowed feverishly, imagining city girls watching him ardently from the beach.

Later enormous bulldozers came and made the dirt road. People talked about tourism, which would make them all rich, and about the "enormous possibilities" in the district, but apart from a handful of peasants who settled in San Jorge nothing changed much. Certainly not his life: the same sea, the same boat, the same beach, the same dances, the same stories, the same girls. Oh, yes, there was one difference: the fish were getting fewer; you had to work harder for less reward. It wasn't exactly prison, but it wasn't much different, either. You did the same things the same way you had always done them, and there didn't seem any way out.

One day, hauling the nets ashore and seething with plans to leave this God-forsaken sandbar for Caracas, he felt someone pulling behind him and turned around. A swarthy, unfamiliar face smiled at him. Pedro smiled back and went on with his work. The nets held three catfish, five groupers, and a porgy.

"Are you passing through?" Pedro asked the stranger.

"I'm visiting my mother's cousin, Señora Isabel." "She's a good woman," said Pedro. "Where you from?"

They had sat down at the water's edge, with the waves splashing their bare feet, watching the water as they talked.

"Originally from Barlovento. Araguita. It's a small village near Caucagua. But for some years now we've been living in Caracas."

Caracas, city of his dreams! Merely living there made the stranger admirable in his eyes. He looked at him with awe and, as if he were talking to himself, murmured wistfully, "How I'd love to live in Caracas." The stranger said nothing. Pedro lowered his head and muttered against the sound of the sea: "It's a dead-end life, living in these little villages."

The stranger only smiled and said, "Life in Caracas is hard. Caracas is a very cruel city." Pedro felt his glittering fantasies begin to shrivel into self-deception under that quizzical smile. Still, he had so nearly persuaded himself of their truth that he could not relinquish them now.

"That doesn't matter to me," he said firmly.

"Better a tough life than this endless boredom. Nothing ever happens here. In Caracas at least you meet new people, you can learn, get ahead." He fiddled for a moment with a lump of damp sand, lingering over the words "Get ahead," which were the kernel of all his dreams. Then, risking the city stranger's derision, he blurted: "Would it be so hard to go and live in Caracas? Do you know of anyone?"

"No, it's not hard. If you want to, come with us."

Pedro was dumbfounded. Was it supposed to be so simple, so attainable? Now that he almost had what he wanted, what was he afraid of—getting it or not getting it?

"Would you really take me? Look, I've got no relatives and I don't know anyone. . . ."

"There's room in my house. I live alone with my mother. You could stay with us till you found a place of your own."

It was simple! Pedro's face lit up. Reeling amid an unaccustomed welter of ideas and emotions, he managed to say, "But wouldn't I be in your way?"

"No, not at all. Don't worry about that. If you want to come. . . ." The man paused. Then he began to speak as if something were hurting him: "But don't think that life in Caracas is easy. People suffer there much more than here. There is no place in the big cities. People seem to become callous and cold-blooded. The only thing that seems to count there is money." He fell silent, brooding, but Pedro felt joyful, almost lightheaded, as if he had not heard a word of the warning.

"What's your name, Sir?" he asked suddenly, holding out his rough hand to the stranger.

"Jesus. And don't call me 'Sir'; it makes me feel pompous. What's yours?"

"Pedro." They shook hands.

"Pedro, you strike me as a truly good person. If you want to come to Caracas, I'd be glad to have you stay with us."

Pedro felt as if his whole life had been waiting for this day. The stranger was not only inviting him to Caracas but telling him he was a specially good person.

He asked, "Do you work, Sir?"

"Yes, I work in a cement factory."

"Do you earn much?"

"No. Very little. Workers earn very little in Caracas."

"But they must earn more than here, Sir. Have you got a car?"

"No, I haven't, and please stop calling me 'Sir.' "

"I'm sorry, Sir—I mean, not—Sir. We're not used to talking to strangers, and city people. . . ."

Pedro stopped. He was imagining himself a "city person," Pedro the City Man, at the wheel of a Cadillac, tearing through Caruao in a cloud of dust, sounding his horn. "Who is the dark, handsome man in the white Cadillac?" asked the girls, crowding into their doorways. "It's Pedro who left for Caracas. He's made a pile of money, but forget about him, sweetheart, he's got a fantastic blonde. . . ."

"Cars and money aren't the most important things." The voice jerked Pedro out of his dreams. How could Jesus have known what he was thinking, and why was he looking at him so probingly?

"What is, then?" he asked very quietly.

"People living like brothers and sisters. Sharing the work and sharing the pay so that nobody starves and nobody gets rich."

Pedro stared at him, frowning. He was an expert on being poor and he could imagine being rich, but sharing he had never heard of and didn't understand.

"How would that work?" he asked himself, kicking the pebbles on the burning sand.

"I'll get some more beer, Pedro said.

Andres and Tomas passed him their empty bottles.

"Three more pints," said Pedro.

Now the juke box was playing, "They're going to get rid of the ugly ones," and a few couples were dancing.

"I haven't seen Jesus around," said the bartender, passing him the bottles.

"He didn't come. He stayed back in Caracas," Pedro answered.

"How are things going there?"

"Well. Very well." Pedro became excited. "Slowly people are waking up. They're getting the idea that they don't have to be kicked around."

The bartender frowned. "You'll all end up in prison if you don't learn to mind your own business and forget about changing the world." His voice quickened: "They're saying that this Jesus has quite a record."

Pedro glared at him. "Are you telling me I should leave him? You know I'm his best friend and I stick with him whatever happens. Even if I get sent to prison with him. Anyway, Caracas people aren't like the people around here. They know what human beings are entitled to and they're willing to fight for it."

Pedro went out with the three bottles without waiting for an answer.

"Always a big mouth," thought the bartender. "When it comes to the crunch he'll run so fast they won't even see his dust."

"Here, drink up fast before it goes warm," said Pedro. Andres and Tomas sat up on the sand. A boy ran past, pulling by the hand a girl in a tiny red bikini.

"Not bad," said Andres.

Tomas nodded without taking the bottle from his lips.

The beach was filling up and the sea seemed louder, as if it were trying to make itself heard above the noise of the people.

"Lousy tourists are going to ruin all these villages," said Andres. "It's not like it was. And when they pave the road the rich will come and then it'll be villas and hotels and to hell with the fishermen."

Tomas lay back on the sand with his eyes closed and began to speak. "But the tourists also bring in some money. They bring business. There are bars and shops in the villages now. That's progress."

"Don't be an idiot," said Andres. "All they bring are their selfishness and their vices. As soon as the road is paved these beautiful beaches will all be private. Then what? You think they'll put up signs saying, 'Smelly fishermen and poor people welcome'?"

"Impossible," said Tomas. "Private beach clubs are against the law."

"You, simp! The rich can get around anything. So it'll be a public beach, but with an entrance fee or a service charge. Whatever they call it, it'll be money, and we won't be able to pay, so good-bye beach. They'll put up showers that everyone has to walk under—for a fee, and everyone will have to wear bathing suits and change their clothes in locker-rooms—for a fee, and the Negro Primero will close and a fancy 'club' will open where a bottle of beer costs ten bolivars. It'll be a free beach, all right, except that even breathing on it will cost money."

"Other places the beach is all fenced, and if you aren't a member or haven't got a ticket you can't get in," said Pedro. "Modesto was telling me that last Sunday he went to Blue Beach with his family and they told him ten bolos or no beach. He told them about the governor's order, and they said order or no order if he wanted to swim there he had to buy a ticket, and they called over a big bouncer-type to see that he got the message. He paid the ten bolos, in spite of the governor's order; it was that or go home."

"Well, naturally," said Andres. "We're not the government. Rich people are the government. You don't expect them to go against themselves—or each other?"

"So if we want to change things, we have to change them for ourselves," said Pedro. "Well, I'm going in. This sun is getting hotter and hotter."

He got up, crashed into the sea at a dead run, and began to swim as though he were racing. He enjoyed feeling the sea slip past him, as if obedient to his strong, regular strokes. The

cool water and his mastery of it filled him with furious ela-
tion, and he swam and swam, away from the beach and the
breakers crashing, out to where the water was blue and
quiet. There he closed his eyes and rolled over on his back to
float and think. . . .

"But it's obvious that Jesus is an extraordinary man." He
still couldn't understand him, after the years they'd been
together. The man was an unknown quantity, as he liked to
tell Judas. Every time he thought he finally understood
him, he got another surprise. On the surface the man was
clear and simple as still water, but deep and complicated
underneath. Peculiar, in some ways. He had no political
sense, as Simon was always telling him. Your ordinary radi-
cal, what he wanted was power to change "the system," but
Jesus couldn't have cared less about power or changing "the
system." Said you had to change people's hearts first—teach
'em to love each other—and then "the system" would
change of itself. Well, if that's what he was waiting for, he'd
wait till hell froze over. Still, he wouldn't take advantage of
ordinary opportunities. If he'd wanted to he could certainly
have gotten on the council, even become mayor or been
elected to congress. But he wouldn't have anything to do
with politicians, saying they were all the same, parrots
screeching out of both sides of their mouths without ever
meaning a word of what they said. He could have had important offices, and used them to do a lot for his own people, but
he wouldn't take them. He wouldn't leave his neighborhood.
He said you had to stick with your class and not be seduced
away from your own people by the temptation to do things
for them instead of *with* them, because it was the people
who were the true agents of liberation. Real changes came
only from below, he said, when the poor people felt and
believed in and lived by their own values. So convinced was
he of these illusions that he would take no decisions, but
waited for the people to show what they wanted—he, who
with one word could have raised every slum-dweller to any
cause he chose. Simon was partly right when he said Jesus

lacked strategy, lacked effectiveness, and that his principles were simply delaying the revolutionary process. But Simon's improvised guerrilla tactics weren't much use either. No short-term gains could make Jesus drop his principles, while Simon grabbed at short-term gains regardless of principles. Somewhere in between was the right way. He, Pedro, would convince Jesus. . . .

Pedro began to swim vigorously back to shore. "But I'll always stay with him," he told himself as he swam. "Even if I never manage to convince him. Where could I go if I left him? I couldn't learn to work with anyone else, not after knowing Jesus. He changes a person."

When he stepped onto the sand with the water dripping off him, his son Pedrito came running.

"Papa, Papa, Mama says we're going to the river now to make fish soup."

VIII

SIMON THE ZEALOT WAS STANDING AT THE TOP OF GOLGOTHA HILL. *It seemed ignoble to look for a patch of shade when his friend was about to die, but the sun's heat beat down on him like a club. He looked at the three newly dug holes on the hilltop, with the sun glancing off the soldier's lance stuck in the center one. Two executioners had pre-empted the only shady place on the hill and were dozing there, their heads resting on their hammers. He could hear the crowd coming closer. Quite a few people were coming on ahead; they would forego accompanying the victims' tortured last walk for the sake of getting good places from which to see them die. They were edgy with anticipation—and because of the presence of the Roman soldier. "Vultures!" thought Simon. "Jackals!" But the epithets were insufficient to his loathing. The beasts were as God had made them, and death, to them, meant only food. But these people—these crawling maggots claiming descent from David and the Maccabees, these poltroons clamoring that Caesar is their only king—they came for the pain and the death. They had no hope—just a little, secret itch that only the pain and death could scratch. No wonder they were abandoned by their God, sold by their priests and leaders, and paralyzed by their fear of the eagles of Rome.*

Simon turned to look at the soldier. The sun, he was glad to see, blazed on Roman as well as Jew: The Roman's face was red with heat and shiny with sweat. But there the resemblance ended, for the Roman was thick with battle-hardened muscle and the sun that made his face red also made his armor gleam. Simon looked at him with hatred and stroked the dagger under his tunic. The feel of it kindled his pride. He, at least, was not afraid. But he looked despairingly as the soldier with one curt gesture cleared the narrow path of people. They recoiled like the tide receding, not looking at the Roman, as though they had themselves intended at the very moment to move aside.

Buffoons! Cowards! He, Simon, could not bear their cowardice. How could they bear themselves? They deserved to go into exile again, to be beaten and bite the dust, like their fathers enslaved in Egypt and Babylon. Only exile and forced labor could remind them of who they were. He gripped the dagger so hard that it hurt him.

The mob-noise was getting close now, and flies were coming in droves, drawn by the sweating bodies.

"He took being beaten without a sound," said a small man beside him who smelled of goat. "I wonder can he keep quiet when they pound the nails in?"

"I think God is in this man," said his companion, who had a large scar on his face and looked immensely sad.

Simon put his head in his hand to hide his agitation. Who, really, was this Jesus? He had been his friend for nearly three years and how little he knew him. . . .

"And he told Pilate he was not a king of this world," continued the small man who smelled of goat. "But that one day soon he would come in power in the clouds." "Yes, I'm sure that God is in this man," answered his friend, and raised his eyes as if he expected already to see supernatural beings approaching on the clouds.

Overhead the sun still shone, but on the horizon dark, heavy clouds were forming.

"There'll be a storm this afternoon," said the man with the scarred face. "If the clouds don't blow away it will pour."

"Hebron dates, Nazareth figs!" cried a fruit-seller. The flies buzzed and settled on his wares.

Simon had joined the Zealots because he could no longer endure the shame of Roman domination. Of course it was

Yahweh's will that Israel should be conquered; clearly it was their punishment for forgetting his law and his covenant. But for all their backsliding Yahweh was their God and they were his people, and that meant their punishment would not be forever. He who had sent the Romans to conquer them would send them a Messiah to lead them into battle and free them. In their long history it had happened many times before and it would happen again: their sin, Yahweh's wrath, his abandoning them to their enemies, and finally his strong hand outstretched for their deliverance. Yahweh, who had sent them Moses and destroyed Pharaoh's armies, would send them a new deliverer and destroy Rome's legions.

Simon remembered the secret meetings where they divided their time between searching the Scriptures for signs of the Messiah's coming and planning sabotage and terror and uprisings against the Romans.

And then he had begun hearing the name Jesus. He didn't remember exactly when or from whom. At first it was just a rumor about a new prophet doing miracles in Galilee. But the rumors multiplied, and soon one met people who had seen him, touched him, heard him speak, and felt themselves reborn. It was then that Simon decided to go and see for himself.

He followed Jesus about for a few days, studying him, never taking his eyes off him. Nights, he pondered everything the man had said and done, but he couldn't make up his mind about him. The man seemed mild-mannered and gentle, but the sight of injustice or oppression could rouse him to sudden, startling fury. He called prostitutes and publicans his friends, and didn't seem to care that the pillars of the community were becoming his enemies. He talked much about "his kingdom," but it was hard to know what he meant by it: it was something to be sown in one's heart; it was like a tiny mustard seed that would grow large; it was like a feast to which the unprepared could not come. It didn't seem to depend in the least on throwing out the

Romans, although it specifically excluded the rich and powerful. It was like no kingdom Simon had ever heard or conceived of.

Simon passed sleepless nights and confused, frustrating days. This Jesus was a superb leader. He had only to let fall a hint for his followers to rise against the Romans. But he didn't seem interested in independence or, in fact, in anything political. Now, if he hadn't come to free them from Rome, could he be the awaited Messiah? But his words and his works all pointed to his being the Messiah. He must be waiting for the right moment to reveal himself, for that day when the number of his followers and their fervor would reach their peak. That had to be the explanation.

So on that blue morning when Jesus spoke his name and asked him to be his friend, Simon's heart was ready to burst. He saw this invitation as a call to become Jesus' captain and lead an army against Rome.

But soon came the disappointments. The afternoon after the miracle of the loaves, when he and the other followers were urging the well-fed masses to acclaim Jesus king, he had disappeared—gone into hiding, with power his for the asking! From that day on all Simon's doubts had reawakened and grown. Jesus' power and popularity were obvious, but it was also obvious that he did not intend to use them as Simon and his friends wished. He told them that those who wanted to rank first in "his kingdom" should serve others, he began speaking of his death as if he longed for it, and one day he castigated his best friend, Peter, for objecting to his talk of death.

Simon raised his head. The crowd had reached the top of the hill. Five Roman soldiers were keeping the area around the post-holes clear with their lances. "Death," thought Simon. "He said that by his death he would establish 'his kingdom.' He said it was necessary for him to die to enter into his glory . . . and that he would return victoriously with legions of angels." The sky had grown queerly dark and ominous looking, and Simon began half to expect a miracle.

Fear and hope revived in his heart, and with them pain—the pain of looking helplessly on while his master and friend was crucified. He thought of stroking his dagger again, but he didn't do it. One of the soldiers was looking at him.

IX

"Good soup," said Tomas. He blew on it to cool it as he ate. Martina, Pedro's wife, looked at him with satisfaction but said nothing. She served her brother-in-law Andres a brimming plateful.

"Tell Pedrito to come out of the water now and eat," she said to her husband. "What a child! I can never get him out of the water."

Pedro walked to the riverbank. Even to his calloused feet the stones were burning hot. "Come out now, Pedrito, and come eat," he called, in his best stern-father voice. The child dived and swam under water to the shore. He came out smiling, a small, sturdy, gleaming-wet figure. Pedro put his great hand on the boy's shoulder in a rough caress and smiled without looking at him. He was afraid he might disgrace himself by weeping with love.

"After all that swimming you must be hungry as a tiger. Your mother has made a very good soup," he said to the child.

"I'm going to eat two big bowls full," said the boy, suddenly feeling his stomach churn with hunger. "When we're finished, can we swim again, papa?"

"Yes," said Pedro, "but not right away. You could get cramps and drown from swimming on a full stomach. We'll rest awhile and then we'll swim again."

They ate sitting in a semicircle around the steaming kettle, facing the river. A stand of cans shaded them from the sun.

Absorbed in the pleasures of eating, they hardly spoke. They looked out unseeingly at the river and heard without listening the sound of the water flowing, the light breeze sighing through the cane, and the voices of other people along the beach.

"Pity Jesus couldn't come," said Pedro into the contented silence. "He loves fish soup."

Pedrito stopped eating and looked at his father for a moment. But he spoke to his mother: "Why didn't Jesus come, mama? Why didn't he come?"

His mother looked into his eyes and spoke very gently: "He couldn't, son. He had a lot of very important things to do in Caracas."

Pedrito thought how wonderful it would be if Jesus were there to swim with him and "make a bridge" with his legs for Pedrito to dive under. Then after they had eaten he would tell him the names of the trees and of the birds that flashed across and flew in and out of the cane thicket. He remembered how Jesus had taught him to swim by putting him in the deep part of the river where you couldn't see the stones. With Jesus beside him he had felt only a tiny bit afraid. "Wouldn't it have been good if Jesus could have come, mama?" said Pedrito.

"Yes, son, it would have. But don't worry, you'll see him tomorrow."

"Is Jesus coming tomorrow?" asked the child, his eyes alight with joy.

"No, he isn't. We're going back to Caracas."

"Why so soon, mama?" All the joy went out of the day at such news, and all the merriment out of the dark eyes in the small face.

"We've got to go to church, son. To keep promises and go in procession. These days are too holy to spend by the river just enjoying ourselves."

"And why are they holy, mama?"

His mother hesitated a moment before answering: "Because during these days, many years ago, they killed God."

She got up to refill Tomas's plate.

"Not too much," said Tomas, "I'll burst."

"Don't be shy. As if we don't all know that you're a bottomless pit."

Pedrito began eating again fast, but his eyes were full of questions. This time he turned to his father, whose eyes were fixed on the cane thicket.

"Papa, is it true what mama says? Is it true they killed God? Why did they?—Hey, papa, why did they kill God?"

Pedro heard his son's voice beside him. He did not answer.

"Because he was very good," he heard Andres answering, the words coming out muffled through a mouthful of fish.

"Bad people hated him, so they killed him," said Filomena, Andres's wife. "It was many years ago. You haven't finished your food, child."

"You told me you were going to eat two big bowls full," said Pedro, leaning toward his son.

Pedrito started eating more quickly. When he had finished he held out his plate to his mother, and smiling triumphantly, asked for more.

"If he was good, why did they kill him? Did they kill good people then?"

"Yes, son," said Pedro. "And they still do. There've always been and always will be very bad people in the world, who only care about their own comforts and the rest of the world can go hang. But these people don't think of themselves as bad, and they don't want to hear it from anyone else either. They're rich people, important people, and they're so used to having everyone suck up to them that they end up killing anyone who dares to tell them to their faces how bad they are, anyone who tells them that having too much is a sin, anyone who defends the poor. That's why they killed God's son. Now you know."

Pedrito listened spellbound. Terror was welling up in him, and the moment his father finished speaking he cried out, "But they won't kill Jesus, will they?"

"Pedrito, what are you talking about? Why should they kill Jesus?" asked Martina in a frightened voice.

"God in heaven, what a thing to think of!" added Filomena.

"Because he is good and defends the poor. Papa said that even now they still kill good people. Will they kill Jesus too?"

The child began weeping with fear for his friend. Pedro moved close to him and held him tightly. He could feel his son's heart beating fast and the little, sturdy body shivering and shaking.

"No, son, no. Nobody's going to do anything to Jesus. Don't worry. Everybody likes him."

The child quietened in his father's arms.

"So here in Venezuela there aren't any of those bad people who kill good people?" he asked, begging his father for reassurance.

"No, son, there aren't."

The shivering and sobbing subsided. Papa had said it, so it must be true. Besides, he wanted to believe it and not be frightened for Jesus any more. He smiled tentatively, wriggled out of his father's arms, and returned hungrily to his soup.

"What we need now is a drink," said Andres, rummaging in an old Munich Olympics sports bag. He brought out a bottle containing a dark amber liquid and showed it to them with satisfaction. Pedro's eyes lit up.

"Yes, a drink and then a siesta to sleep off our lunch," he said, rubbing his full stomach.

They all drank, the women too, passing the rum from one to the other and slurping directly from the bottle.

"Good stuff," said Tomas with conviction.

"You can go and play now, son, but don't go into the water," said Martina to Pedrito.

"If you bring me that stick I'll make you a fishing rod. I brought you a hook," said Tomas to the child.

Pedrito watched fascinated and happy as Tomas fastened a nylon cord with a hook on the end of it to the rod.

"We haven't got any worms, so we'll put a bit of bread on the hook," Tomas told him.

"Do fishes like bread too?" asked the child, watching him bury the hook in a lump of bread.

"Yes, they do. Not as much as worms, but they do like it. You'll see how they bite. Cast the hook in the deep water, now that nobody is swimming. Look, take this bread and when the fish have eaten the other bit, put pieces of it on the hook to hide it, like you saw me doing."

"If they see the hook they don't bite?"

"No, they don't. These fish are very clever."

All was well with the world again. The sky looked very high and bright, the sun was hot, but the cane grew down to the very edge of the river and shaded it, and where the river was deep the muddy water ran slower and quieter. Pedrito made his cast as his father had taught him and settled himself hopefully to wait.

"What would Judas be doing now?" asked Pedro, lying on his back with his eyes closed.

Nobody answered, so in the silence Pedro expanded his question: "He didn't want to come either. He says it is wrong to go to the beach on holy days. He takes religion too seriously."

"He doesn't know how to enjoy life," said Tomas. "He always seems tied in knots."

"But he's a good man, only fanatical," said Andres, yawning.

They were silent again, lying on the shaded sand and hearing the river lulling them to sleep.

"I don't like Judas. I don't know why, but sometimes he scares me," said Martina with a slight quaver in her voice.

"Don't talk nonsense, woman," interrupted Pedro. "You and your intuitions! What's to be afraid of? Judas is better and more upstanding than any of us."

"His eyes are shifty—always darting around," Martina went on. "Lately he acts strange, as if he weren't our friend. As if he didn't trust us. He seems unhappy. And when he's with Jesus he won't look at him—or anyone."

"It's his religious training," said Andres. "He didn't use to be like that. These courses that he takes put all kinds of

strange ideas into his head. He sees Communists everywhere."

"I don't know what it is," said Martina. "But I know Judas
scares me. Because of Jesus and all of us."

Pedro opened his mouth to contradict her but said nothing.
It was too much of an effort to speak when he felt so drowsy.
Everybody was silent and he could hear the sound of the
river.

Pedrito hauled in his line. The fishes were smart, like
Andres said. They had eaten every piece of bread off his
hook and not one had he caught. He wound the line round
the rod and went back to his parents, looking troubled again.
He made no sound as he came, and his parents did not
wake when he stood looking down at them. His father was
breathing heavily in his sleep, almost snoring. Then he
grabbed his mother's feet. Martina opened her eyes and saw
the trouble in his face. She drew him down to her.

"Didn't catch anything?" she asked very softly.

The child did not reply.

"Aren't there rich people in Venezuela, mama?" he asked,
looking worriedly into her eyes.

"Of course, silly, there are rich people in Venezuela.
There are rich and poor people everywhere."

"And isn't it true that Jesus stands up for the poor?"

"Yes, son, Jesus is friendly with the poor."

"But the rich people won't do anything to Jesus, will
they?"

"No, son, why should they do anything?"

"Because he stands up for the poor. Papa said that they
killed God because he defended the poor."

"Yes, but we told you, that was a long time ago."

"So the rich people in Venezuela now aren't bad?"

"No, they're not. Sleep a little. Rest."

"If the rich people aren't bad, why are there so many poor
people?"

"The child has had too much sun," said Filomena very
quietly. "He must have a fever. Feel his forehead."

Pedrito seemed not to have heard. He was watching his
mother.

"So, mama, if they aren't bad, why do there have to be poor people?"

"Well, in fact the rich people aren't very good people. They aren't either good or bad. They're just ordinary. They're not bad enough to kill anybody but not good enough to want there to be no more poor people. Now sssh, son. Everyone's asleep and you'll wake them up."

"Jesus once told me that there are very bad people here who have a lot of money but won't give any of it to poor people even when they have nothing to eat, that they waste their money on junk or keep it in the bank and don't care about anybody."

"Yes, that's true, but they aren't bad enough to kill anybody. The world has changed a lot."

There was a pause. The child closed his eyes and opened them again, seeking his mother's face.

"And if they want to kill Jesus will papa protect him?"

"Of course he will, son, and so will we all. Stop worrying and sleep now. Everybody loves Jesus and nobody's going to hurt him."

Pedro had been listening, pretending to be asleep. He didn't want to say anything. He went on listening till his wife and child were quiet. Then heat and sleep overcame him again.

X

"BE QUIET. I don't want to hear about it any more. We are not going to the beach. Is that clear? If you want to swim and sunbathe you can go to the pool in Caracas. The sun shines there too."

Dr. Linares, Chairman of the Board of Linares Industries, Incorporated, an ever growing conglomerate that seemed, to some prejudiced observers, coterminous with the national economy, was annoyed. His normally smooth plump face was furrowed with temper. He took a longer than usual sip of whiskey and turned back to his paper.

"Don't be like that," said his wife soothingly, lifting her soft green eyes from her magazine. "It's only natural for the boy to be disappointed at having to spend his vacation here. All his friends have gone away. Don't forget that you were young once too."

Dr. Linares made a valiant effort to calm down. He managed to disperse some of the wrinkles.

"Of course I understand. But he ought to make a bit of an effort to understand too. After all, he isn't a child any longer."

Seeing that his father was calmer and his mother—at least tacitly—was on his side, Roberto tried again.

"Yes, but at Camuri they are only going to let members in. Clive told me. His father telephoned before he left and it was definite. If you don't believe me, phone and ask them yourself."

"I've told you we're not going, and that's that! So don't start about telephoning all over the place. We're not going.

Understand?" And having delivered this final salvo, Dr. Linares retired again behind the impregnable wall of his newspaper. Roberto controlled his tears of rage by staring hard at the tips of his shoes. Then he glanced appealingly at his mother.

"If it's true what the boy says, and we make sure beforehand . . . ?" she hazarded placatingly.

"There are all kinds of risks," began Dr. Linares in a carefully restrained voice. "The situation is very uncertain. Do you think I haven't made inquiries? It's true that for the moment the governor's order does not seem to have affected our beach, but who's to say that the idiot won't go all the way in one of his bursts of demagoguery? Politician! Fool!" He paused, chewing over all the other epithets that would apply to the governor. It was a long list, and it would have pleased him to say them all to the governor, but the governor wasn't there.

"Bring me more ice," he ordered Roberto.

"Me? What do we have servants for?" He had to get back at his father somehow, even if he was punished for it.

Dr. Linares disliked insubordination, from employees or children, and he was accustomed to punish it, but his wife hastened to intervene.

"Juana," she called, "bring the Señor some ice cubes."

With his father's eyes glaring at him, Roberto felt like crying again. Deliberately he scuffed the polished floor with the heel of one shoe and went out banging the door behind him.

"You shouldn't treat him like that. He's very upset, and that's quite understandable," remonstrated his mother. Her face was still unlined and smooth as a model's, although she was over forty.

Dr. Linares said nothing while the maid put a bowl of ice down beside him.

"Anything else, Sir?" she asked, with a curtsey she had learned from the movies.

"No, thank you," said the Doctor.

"Anything for you, Madam?"

"Will you boil the water for tea, please."

"He'll get over it," said Dr. Linares when the maid had gone out. "He's got nothing to complain about. Let him go to the swimming pool with his sisters."

"But you know he has nothing to do there. He feels lonely; none of his friends are in town."

Dr. Linares shrugged.

"Yes, yes, I understand. It's not very pleasant for me either, cooped up in the city during my vacation, but there's nothing else to be done."

His wife turned on him her most melting look and spoke in her softest voice.

"But they say that it's still only open to members. . . ."

Dr. Linares's eyes blazed furiously, and the wrinkles came back.

"I've already told you that there is a risk the beach will be opened to the public. Haven't you ever seen the people on the public beaches? Filthy, half drunk, swilling down their revolting-smelling fish soup, making filthy remarks at all the women and looking as if they're about to rape them. And you want to take your daughters there?"

He paused. His wife was contemplating his description. She looked—finally—appropriately nervous and nauseated.

"And there's something else," continued Dr. Linares, "that I didn't want to speak about in front of the boy. Even if our beach still is restricted, what's to prevent the mob from simply forcing its way in? God knows they've had enough demagogues and rabble-rousers telling them it's their right! And if they did break in, they'd be in the mood for any kind of atrocity. Do you want to be there—with your daughters— when it happens?"

By now his wife looked really ill. She was imagining the nameless atrocities. "Please stop," she begged. "I don't want to talk about it any more. I'll settle Roberto down and take him with me to see the processions here in town."

Dr. Linares did not reply, and his wife fell silent. She found herself trembling all over at the imagined onslaughts of hordes of huge, filthy, faceless, dark-skinned men who reeked of beer and fish and old sweat. She rose and left the room. She needed a real bath to cleanse her body of the imagined vileness.

She came back wearing fresh clothes from the skin out and smelling of cologne. By her chair was a steaming cup of tea and a plate of unsalted biscuits.

"Oh, I forgot to tell you," she said to her husband, biting delicately into a biscuit, "Juana asked me if she could have two or three days off to go home to her village. You know how sentimental they are about holy days."

Dr. Linares looked up again from his paper. His expression was hard.

"I hope you told her no. Especially now that we have to stay here at home."

"You try talking to her. She seemed sad."

"Pay her a bit extra. That'll cheer her up." Dr. Linares tried to find his place again. At this rate he would never finish the article on inflation he was reading.

The silence that followed clacked and buzzed with their unspoken thoughts. Suddenly Dr. Linares realized he had not absorbed a single word that he had read. He passed a hand across his face as if he were removing a spider's web and snapped: "As if it didn't cost anything to keep up private beaches. It was our money that converted them from barrens into beaches. And now comes this demagogue with all kinds of laws and regulations to open them to his beloved 'public.' It would be funny if it weren't a real possibility. Living in the governor's mansion must have gone to his head."

That such an important man should be so petulant, his wife thought. Perhaps there were issues she couldn't see. There usually were, according to her husband. But if she didn't always see the issues, she did know a woman's duty, and that was to look good, smell good, and speak soothingly. As soon as her husband stopped for breath she did her duty.

"He won't last long if he goes on doing such ridiculous things."

"Mummy, I'm dying of boredom. Why can't we go somewhere?" groaned Nancy, at that moment appearing at the patio door. She had eyes like her mother's, only blue, and her freshly brushed hair was dark blond, streaked with the sun that had tanned her skin the color of toast. A tiny red bikini set off to perfection her fashionable adolescent figure.

"You know your father has said that we are not going anywhere," said her mother, pretending to be angry in order to avert her husband's anger.

"But what is there to do here shut up in this prison? What a holiday! Solitary confinement!"

She flung herself into a yellow armchair, looking as if she was going to cry.

It was odd, her father thought, that he could never get as irritated with his pretty daughter as with his son, even when they did and said the same things.

"Look, sweetheart, try and understand. I've already explained to you why we can't go to the beach this year. Try and amuse yourself here as best you can. You've got the swimming pool, books, records, television. . . . You can go to the movies later if you like. Think of all the girls who dream of being able to spend vacations like yours."

"Yes, there's the swimming pool, but it's boring alone. And the same with listening to records. And I'm sick of television and I read all the books anyone could stand in school. What's the point of having six new bikinis if I'm shut up like a nun in a convent!" At the thought of her pitiful predicament, a few tears welled up and rolled down her cheeks. Then she went on: "I don't see why we can't go to the beach too, even if all those other people did come. After all, what are they going to do to us?"

"Be quiet, child, be quiet." Her mother was genuinely agitated. "You don't know what you're talking about. Because you have no idea what could happen doesn't mean that nothing would happen."

"At least we could have gone to Miami or someplace. All my friends have gone to fun places and I'm stuck here like an idiot. What will I tell them when we go back to school? Oh, *we* spent *our* vacation in beautiful downtown Caracas!"

She began to cry again noisily now at the thought of the

inevitable humiliation awaiting her. Her mother went to her and stroked her hair.

"Don't be like that, Nancy, calm down. Your father has done everything he could. I was with him when he was phoning all the airlines. He wanted to give us a surprise but he couldn't get tickets. All the flights were booked."

"Of course he couldn't get tickets! How are you going to get tickets at vacation-time at the last minute? If he'd wanted to go away he'd have booked seats in advance, but he loves staying home stuffing himself and doing nothing, so he doesn't see why that's not good enough for the rest of us."

"Hush," said her mother emphatically. Without looking she could see her husband's wrinkles deepening into furrows on his brow. She stopped trying to soothe her daughter and simply repeated: "Be quiet, child, be quiet. You don't know what you're talking about."

Dr. Linares had been listening, saying nothing. Now he exploded and shouted: "Leave her alone, let her snivel her head off! She's so goddamned spoiled she doesn't know what she wants. If she's bored let her go to work."

At her father's failure to feel guilty, and at the outrageousness of his last suggestion, Nancy's grief overwhelmed her. She cried hysterically, fending off her mother's caresses, and ran gulping and sobbing to lock herself in her room.

"You shouldn't have said that to her," her mother ventured.

"I'm fed up with all the complaining and I don't want any more of it." It was his business voice, harsh and domineering. "You all forget that I've got the right to rest too."

Complete silence. Neither of them knew where to look, or how to reestablish even an appearance of coolness and contentment. Goddamn the 'public'! They spoiled everything just by existing.

The telephone rang, sounding very loud in the silence, and the señora rose gratefully to answer it.

"It's for you," she said to her husband. "Briceno."

"Hello, Briceno. Linares here. What's new?" His voice was extra loud and confident, and his eyes focused on the middle distance, as they always did when he took business calls. Maybe this would expunge that distasteful scene with his wife and children. He could hear Briceno's voice at the end of the line, sounding remote and distorted.

"Sir, I forgot to tell you that as was agreed at the last managers' meeting, we fired the employees Jesus Rodriguez and Felipe Peres, his sidekick. We paid their wages and told them we had no further need of their services."

Dr. Linares listened expressionlessly. He could imagine Briceno's small eyes and waxy complexion at the end of the line. Metallic clouds were forming outside, and the afternoon darkened.

"Do you think that might cause any problem?" he asked tonelessly.

"No, I don't think there is anything to worry about. Fortunately, we were in time. They were just getting their union off the ground. The men aren't organized enough to be able to make trouble. They don't even want to—all they care about is keeping their jobs. Now that we've gotten rid of the leaders, what do the others know about 'class consciousness' or 'workers' rights'? Anyway, with the Easter holiday coming they'll forget all about it."

A smile that was more of a grimace spread over Dr. Linares's face. He looked at the clock on the far wall and saw it would soon be six.

"Anything else about this Jesus?" he asked without much interest, sounding suddenly tired.

"Not much more than we knew already. Maybe dangerous; certainly peculiar. Seems he can't be bought. You know the type: a cross between a puritan fanatic and a mulish peasant. No one has ever caught him on the take—either for money or for his own power. I've heard he's turned down some local offices. Hard to tell if he's for real or just very, very clever. The people in his neighborhood think highly of him but I don't know how many really support all his ideas. All kinds of politicians have tried to co-opt him, but nobody's succeeded yet. He has quite a police record too, and there's a rumor that he has contacts with the extreme left. He talks a lot about equality and justice and brotherhood. So he may be a fanatic or he may be a champion con artist or he may be just a harmless, deluded dreamer."

"But even dreamers—with his kind of dreams—can cause a lot of trouble," interrupted Dr. Linares. "They never keep quiet, and they get people dangerously worked up. They have to be stopped."

"Yes, that's true, Sir. That's why I think the dismissal was a good thing. He can't stir up our men, and being out of work will give him something to think about besides brotherhood."

"Make sure none of our associates hires him."

"Of course, Dr. Linares, his name has already been circulated to all the offices."

"Well, I congratulate you on a good job," said Dr. Linares, obviously wanting to end the conversation. "Are you going anywhere for the holiday?"

"Yes, yes. We're leaving this evening, in fact. That's why I phoned now. I'm going to Seville with my wife for a few days. You know what the Good Friday processions are like there, and she enjoys that sort of thing. And you, Sir?"

"It seems we're going nowhere. We had planned to go to the beach as we've done for the last few years, but our dear Governor Bleeding-Heart has ruined that." Dr. Linares was unconscious of the change in his voice. The mere mention of going anywhere had turned the captain of industry back into the unfairly beset, infuriated husband and father.

There was silence at the other end of the line and in the room. Briceno was obviously framing a diplomatic reply and Señora Linares was looking volumes but saying nothing aloud.

"Yes, Sir, these populist games will be the ruin of the country," said the voice on the telephone, finally.

Fool! thought Dr. Linares savagely. Do *I* need *you* to tell me I'm right? What I need is someone to *do* something about it! "These populist games will be the ruin of him," he said darkly, after a pause. "Anyway, have a good holiday. Goodbye. Regards to Julie."

He hung up.

"We've fired the trouble-maker I was telling you about the

other day. It seems making trouble wherever he goes is his career. But I think he's going to find his opportunities more and more limited," he said to his wife. Then, as if he had suddenly remembered something important, he added, "Don't forget we've got the Monsignor coming to dinner tonight."

"Don't worry. Everything's ready," said his wife. "Let's just hope the children will have calmed down by then."

XI

"BUT MONSIGNOR MUST AT LEAST AGREE WITH ME that the situation is becoming chaotic." Dr. Linares paused, looked at his placidly chewing dinner guest, and continued in a weighty voice.

"People go around publicly spouting insane ideas about social order, and the Church says nothing, which is the same as permitting it. Tell me, doesn't ecclesiastical or canon law provide any sanctions or disciplinary measures against these priests who spend their time 'playing revolution' like adolescents instead of performing their priestly duties? The whole country is crawling with them. They spring up like mushrooms, and wherever they are they make trouble. I think—and don't say I'm wrong—that you Church authorities have a special duty and particular responsibility. If you don't act and act quickly it could be too late."

"It's true that real Christians no longer know what to believe. It's terrible. Every day new things crop up and they all seem so contradictory. . . ." Señora Linares's voice was soft, delicate, breathy, and it trailed off on a questioning note, as though an appeal might elicit the response that her husband's ponderous assertiveness had failed to receive.

"Don't worry so, my friends," said the voice of the Church finally, having first delicately wiped his lips with his napkin. "Exaggerating the problem isn't the same as dealing with it." The Church is already taking appropriate steps, but without haste, without alarm. Those you call priests with a taste for revolution are a tiny minority. Some of them are incompetent

77

theologians who should never have been graduated from the seminary. And nearly all of them are foreigners. They see Venezuela with foreign eyes and foreign expectations, and so they see what doesn't exist. It's unfortunate but inevitable—so few of our own sons feel called to the priesthood that we must depend partly on foreign clergy."

Only toward the end did Monsignor's voice become human. His opening sentences sounded bland and blank, as if they were formulas he had repeated many times before. Dr. Linares had listened carefully, a chunk of lobster poised forgotten on his fork. When he replied it was in an even more worried tone.

"Yes, that's all true, but I don't see it as a cause for optimism. I don't believe they are so few or so insignificant. And in any case only a few are enough to spread confusion and stir up the young hotheads. Besides there are plenty of professional revolutionaries who like nothing better than a bunch of clerical cats-paws to front for them. And we know very well what they want. Look, Monsignor, look at what happened in Chile. We know that communists subverted and used the clergy there, and what was the result? The Allende government! As long as the Church does not disown and silence these Red priests, people will believe them simply because they are priests. Must we have an Allende regime here before the Church acts?"

Señora Linares shuddered delicately. "Please," she said, "I don't even want to think about it," and she crossed her arms defensively over her expensive décolletage.

"I repeat: Don't worry so, my friends." The lobster having been quite consumed during his host's peroration, Monsignor attacked the sirloin with mushroom sauce. "Our situation, thank God, is quite different from Chile's. Moreover, our people have learned their lesson from the Chilean disaster. The results of the last elections showed that conclusively. Venezuela is a very Christian country, and this alone immunizes even the ignorant and unsophisticated against Marxist ideas. Although I grant you there are certain things, particularly at the popular level, that need adjusting."

Dr. Linares was distressed. Monsignor made so little of the

problem. Clearly he didn't understand, or didn't want to understand, the gravity of the situation. Even the bishops seemed to be wearing rose-colored glasses. A guest must be shown every courtesy, particularly a member of Holy Church, but Monsignor was disparaging his warnings, and he, Dr. Linares, was not accustomed to being taken lightly.

"Yes, yes," he said, his irritation showing, "but it would be better to cut out the cancer before it spreads any further. Let's not forget that prevention is always better than cure. There are even priests who go so far as to support unions and strikes; they take factory jobs and turn docile laborers into trouble-makers. The other day, in the Central University itself, a parish priest, a certain Father Juan, stood up and said that religion should be an arm of revolution and that being a Christian means fighting capitalism, and more along the same line. I don't understand why you appear to take no notice. The evil is spreading with the speed of light. I insist, Monsignor, for the good of the country and the Church itself, that you take drastic steps. Canon law must include sanctions for cases like this. . . ."

"At least the Church should tell us what to think about all these new ideas," said Señora Linares with animation. There were the faintest traces of very pale lipstick on her glass. "What troubles me most is not knowing what is Christian and what isn't."

"I tell you again, you make too much of things. The Church's position has been made perfectly clear in a constant flow of documents. As for this Father Juan you mention, Doctor, we all know who he is—a demagogue and a neurotic who expresses his neurosis by talking revolution. The Church will handle him appropriately, you may rest assured. And in any case his maunderings couldn't convince anyone worth convincing."

The sirloin was excellent. Monsignor asked for just a bit more, "Just a mouthful to feel absolutely perfect but not too full." Juana served him. She was appropriately dressed in her evening uniform, and she curtsied and smiled at him, but nobody looked at her.

"Maybe," Dr. Linares retorted, "but nevertheless he

sounds stirring and inspiring to all the young hotheads, or he plays into the hands of professional revolutionaries, who point to him and say, 'Look, the Church is on our side.' You would do well to pay attention to me, Monsignor; being in business makes one a realist. Only yesterday one of our factories fired a local agitator, a Jesus Somebody-or-Other. Shall I tell you something, Monsignor? This man, who lives in Gramoven, or whatever his neighborhood is called, claims that he gets his revolutionary philosophy from the Gospel itself. And you seem to think such a person should be left alone, and that people who never even got through primary school should be allowed to set themselves up as preachers."

Monsignor swallowed a final mushroom and finished his wine. He wiped his lips with his napkin slowly and deliberately. He was beginning to feel irritated with his host— dinner had been excellent but laymen should not set themselves in judgment over Church policies.

"Obviously," he said, "professional agitators will use for their own ends phrases from the Gospel, which they quote quite out of context and without knowing what they really mean. But remember that Christianity is more than a few days old. There have always been heretical movements that tried to use the Gospel as a weapon of revolution. The Middle Ages were full of them. And what came of them? Precisely nothing. Most of them died a natural death. The rest Mother Church put down in her own good time. That's why I say not to worry so much. History repeats itself. We must consider our problems with a certain sense of history. It gives us a reassuring depth of vision. Furthermore, our people know that religion is not learned in factories and on street corners but in church from ordained priests and professional theologians. The people are not as stupid as they may seem to you, Dr. Linares. They aren't deceived so easily. That's why we don't have to dignify agitators and revolutionaries with our concern. The law and the secular authorities can take care of them. You proved the truth of that yourself when you told me about that Jesus from Gramoven.

You pegged him as an agitator, you dismissed him from his job, and that's that. What need for the Church to concern itself with such a creature?"

"Yes, agreed. But that happened precisely because we keep on top of such people, because we are much more realistic than you. Can you deny that it is your duty to condemn publicly all who use Christianity as a banner for revolt and anarchy? At the very least you should keep reminding the faithful of the ecclesiastical condemnations of Marxism and all kinds of socialism. By your noble silence you are letting Christianity become the property of these dialectical adventurers, these Marxists in Christian clothing!"

"They say," added Señora Linares, as though confirming everything her husband had said, "that in Cuba they have turned the churches into dance halls."

"Venezuela offers no opportunities to Marxism or its allies," said Monsignor, sounding dogmatic and by now greatly irritated. "The Church has stated its position clearly and often. Real Christians know what they should think."

"But that is precisely the point I wanted to raise," said Dr. Linares quietly. "We have the feeling—pardon me for being so frank—that your documents and statements are not reaching the people who need to be convinced. The 'real Christians,' as you call them, do know what to think; it's the common people I'm concerned about. The Church may proclaim its views from the pulpit and publish them in *Religion* magazine, but how many of the people who are most easily led astray by Marxism go to church regularly or read *Religion*? What is urgently needed is a popular campaign— no subtleties, no complexities, no discussion of fine points of difference, just an out-and-out condemnation of all forms of socialism as communism in disguise. The need is all the more pressing now, because the Government itself is playing footsie with the left and polishing its populist image, and if the politicians continue this game they will bring this country to the edge of the abyss. But I don't want to argue about the present Government, which I know you support. I assume you know of the recent unofficial conference of businessmen in Rio de Janeiro? And their conclusion that the major problem today in Latin America is the communist clergy and their spies? To fight this danger and give you the opportunity to bring about a genuine renewal of Christian values, my colleagues and I thought of offering the use of the mass media—the popular press, radio, television. . . . We could finance articles . . . programs . . . even a TV series. What do you think?"

Monsignor attacked the strawberry torte. He was thinking, in fact, that his friends were seeing too many demons lurking where they did not exist. At least for the moment there was no danger of communism in Venezuela, especially not with the present government. It could cope with the agitators. The Church was quite all right as it was, without getting mixed up in political and economic problems. Its mission was spiritual. Moreover it should not align itself with the extreme right, because quite clearly the excesses of capitalism and the consumer society were not Christian either, when there were still so many poor people living in wretched conditions. The cake was excellent, and Juana was serving the brandy. The Church, thought Monsignor, should not be tied to anybody. Only to God.

"Armagnac, please," said Monsignor to the maid.

Pilate raised his pale hand to silence the mob. He looked tired and vexed. This interminable and ridiculous case was beginning to wear him out. He knew the priests and community leaders were whipping up the people to demand the death penalty. "If you want blood you shall have it, but that does not mean I must agree to the killing of an innocent man," he thought and ordered the trumpeter to call for silence again. The sound of the trumpet asserted itself over the many voices of the crowd, and the people quieted and turned their eyes toward Pilate. So many eyes, dark and hard. Pilate got up quickly and began pacing up and down with the eyes following him, which gave him an agreeable sense of his power. Then he looked at the accused whom they called the Christ. He stood there dressed as a madman, as Herod had commanded. That was to show that the man was a poor visionary, deluded but not criminal. No, he did not look like a criminal. Even the centurion had informed him that, when arrested, he had surrendered without resistance and had stopped the friends who had tried to defend him. Neither had any specific charges been made that warranted the death penalty. He would never understand these Jews —how could they have adulated this poor zany so wildly, and why did they hate him so fiercely now, just a few days later? Any man of sense could see that he deserved neither the adulation nor the hatred. But then, who ever called Jews sensible? But if they wanted blood he would give them the guerrilla Barabbas, who was really dangerous as he had proved by ambushing a Roman patrol. Yes, that was the solution. He would give them Barabbas and release this poor fool after a cautionary beating to rid him of his extraordinary ideas. Or at least make him keep them to himself. These Jewish priests should not have their way with the poor zany. It was he who dispensed justice here, Roman justice, and if they had forgotten that, they would do well to be reminded.

Pilate stood still in the center of the praetorium. He smiled slightly before he began to speak, in the thin fluting voice that was the subject of so many dirty jokes in the local taverns.

"Herod himself sent him to me having found no reasons to condemn him. Look at him. He is a poor madman, not a criminal. I sentence him to be beaten and then freed."

He raised his arms to quell the growing uproar and show that he hadn't finished yet. He raised his voice: "Barabbas will be executed, who has committed crimes enough to deserve many deaths."

His words acted on the crowd like stones flung at a beehive. For some time it was impossible to hear anything. Everyone was speaking and shouting at once. The centurion looked at Pilate, who looked the accused man in the eyes.

And from the back of the square arose a cry that drowned all the others: "We don't want Barabbas to die. We want this man. Crucify him! Crucify him!"

The cry became one single, tremendous, fanatical deafening voice.

"Crucify him! Crucify him! Crucify him!" Pilate looked at the accused, whose inward-turned gaze had not shifted or changed. It was as if he did not hear them roaring for his death. Pilate had never been fond of Jews—he didn't know any Romans who were—but he had never hated them as he did now.

"Have you nothing to say?"

The accused did not answer, but he did look him in the eyes. Pilate turned away, back toward the mob.

"He has done nothing to deserve death," he shouted, but his words were drowned in the shrieks of the crowd. He ordered the centurion to form up his men in single line in front of the praetorium, and at the sight of the legionaries the cries diminished.

Pilate sat down in the procurator's chair and looked at the people, quelling their uproar with his eyes.

"He shall be scourged and then freed," he said dryly. There was no reply from the mob. Pilate smiled.

"If you release him you are no friend of Caesar's. We'll let Caesar know that you conspire against him by releasing rebels and enemies of Rome."

Pilate rose, the better to see who had spoken. It was a small, lean man in priestly garments. Now other voices in the crowd took up the threat.

"That's it. We'll send a message to Caesar in Rome."

"If you release this man you are a traitor, an enemy of Rome."

"Traitor! Long live Caesar!"

"Long live Caesar in Rome!"

He was outmaneuvered, and he knew it. It was a cheap trick, shabby and transparently false, but not too transparent to convince an emperor who needed no prompting to see conspirators everywhere. Rome was far away and had

enough trouble with uprisings without one of its own gov-
ernors preventing the execution of a rebel condemned by his
own people. His career was on the line, his petition for
transfer to Dalmatia, where the people were more amenable
than these wretched Jews. And if their 'message' reached
Caesar on a nervous day, his life could be on the line as well.
'Recalled to Rome for consultation': a bland formula for an
ominous possibility. There was nothing to be done. He
looked at the accused and shrugged resignedly. He had done
all he could.

Pilate called for water and washed his hands in front of
the people. "I am innocent of the blood of this just man. Do
what you like with him." It was the legal formula. Then he
withdrew. He could hear the mob shrieking with joy. He felt
depressed, partly because he had sent an innocent man to
crucifixion, but more because he had permitted himself to
be outmaneuvered by his inferiors.

XII

Jesus got up quietly in the familiar dark.

"Where are you going, son? Can't you sleep?" The small sounds of his deft, careful movements were enough to reassure her that he was no longer sad.

Jesus smiled in the darkness.

"I'm going out for some fresh air," he said. "It's stuffy. You sleep."

"You're sleeping very little these days. Is anything wrong? You're not sick, are you?"

"No, don't worry. I feel fine. I'm just going out to think a bit."

He went out into the dark and sat down on a flat rock at the edge of the dirt track. He could feel the night breathing, black, deep, and alive, and he stretched out his hand to touch it. The night huddled beside him; he could hear the silence of sleep in all the houses. Below him the brightly lit highway cut through the darkness. Very few cars were going down it, nearly all were coming up. Jesus imagined the people's faces, bronzed by the sea breeze and the sun, the sharp smell of Coppertone, and the aching burns of the shoulders of the overconfident. He sat awhile, thinking nothing, watching the lights below. Slowly he became aware that his breath was laboring and that sorrow lay on his chest like a stone. He raised his eyes to the dying stars and whispered: "Father." The world was inhuman, men glared at each other, love was a helpless quadriplegic. Power used to inflict pain (and gotten by inflicting pain), spilled blood, mindless laughter, hunger, slums, hell in jackboots trampling over the dying land. Jesus wanted to pray but could not. Again the word "Father" trembled on his lips. The city glittered below him. Buildings raised on corpses, inhabited by monsters of egoism, automatons of blind ambition and unconscious malevolence who had once been men.

Dehumanized vampires buried under a mound of possessions, delusions, and greed. The living dead: grimaces for smiles, guffaws for laughter, gold teeth and fetid breath, servicing each other, cannibalizing each other, feeling nothing. And rivers of lies, false promises, futile plans, and sanctimony that annihilates hope. "Why, Lord, why?" He was shaking with horror of it as a man might shake with fever.

He felt old. Tired to death. What was he doing? Why go on shackling his life to his dreams? Could his puny efforts raise up this mountain of inhumanity that was smothering the world? Wasn't it amply clear that the world wasn't going to change? Why couldn't he forget it all and take a little pleasure in life as it was? Why had he been born different?

Loneliness fell upon him. He felt abandoned, without God, without friends, with nothing but pain. He was sweating, and cold from the sweat. He tried to cry, but no tears would come.

A door opened nearby and Madalena came silently out into the night and stood beside him.

"What are you doing, Jesus, at this time of night all alone?"

His head hurt miserably, but her words lightened the darkness. "I was thinking," he replied painfully.

The woman sat down beside him, not speaking but keeping him company in his silence. Jesus could not see her face, but he could feel the affection in her eyes like a poultice on his pain.

"I couldn't sleep either, and I knew that you were out here. . . ."

How much she loved him! Jesus raised his head and

looked through the darkness toward where she sat. He did not speak.

"You're tired, aren't you?" Madalena continued. "Because people—we—hear what you tell us and nothing changes.

Jesus' eyes caressed her for a moment, but Madalena was staring into the dark.

"I get discouraged sometimes. Sometimes my life seems ridiculous. All that hope and all that work and nothing changes. I feel tired. . . . You know I was fired yesterday, and every time it gets harder to find another job. My mother's getting older. She deserves a little ease and comfort. I owe them to her, and I haven't been able to give them to her."

Madalena turned to him and put her hand on his knee. Her hand was thin and trembled slightly, but it had a warmth that spread through him.

"You know that your mother doesn't want anything more than she has. She is proud of you. You love her, and she is proud of that, too. For the rest, don't worry. Your friends are always with you even if they don't always know how to tell you so. It's not true that nothing changes. The people who love you are changed by you, and I don't know anyone who's ever met you who doesn't love you."

She hurried over the last words, because her voice was beginning to break.

"Thank you," said Jesus. "You give me strength. Among my friends I never feel futile."

"Some of us—like me—owe you everything," said Madalena. "You got me out of the life. You taught me to feel happy sometimes. My children love you like you were their father, and I. . . ." Madalena's voice trailed away. Her heart pounded with the words she had bitten back.

"Go back to sleep now and don't torture yourself any more," she said and stood up. "Come and eat at my house tomorrow. Bring your mother, too. I'll invite Judas, Juan, Pedro—it'd be nice to have a little party." She disappeared into the darkness, and Jesus heard her door open and shut softly. He was alone again, looking at his past. He had been sixteen when he dreamt the dream that took hold of his life. For a while he kept on going to night school, but his feeling of the absurdity of life grew till he gave up his plans to enter the university. All people seemed to want was to get and to have—more than each other, more than before—and for this insane and unachievable ambition they gladly destroyed each other. When he had seen this clearly, he pledged himself to try to make the world more human, to be always the ally of those who had nothing. For such a life work, university training was more than unnecessary—it was probably useless. He was convinced that the sick greed to have was what dehumanized people and decided that he would "have" nothing; whatever the world called his would always belong equally to everyone else. And having decided that, he understood instantly that only not-having gives true freedom.

For the most part it had been easy. He had never, even as a child, wanted many things. Only twice the temptation of having had been dangerously strong. Once when he was hitchhiking, a boy and a girl in a convertible stopped.for him. That in itself was unusual; the expensive cars rarely stopped—the drivers were probably afraid you'd rob them, or get the upholstery dirty. But this one stopped for him. The two young people were handsome, with that sheen of well-being that money confers, and the car was fast and smooth and elegantly appointed, and the music from the car radio insinuated itself pleasingly into his thoughts. He had sat in that car, raging at his own folly of not-having and wanting a car like that one and a girl like that one and the full wallet that made having them—having everything and everyone—easy.

They had dropped him at the Barinas crossroads, feeling miserable. For a long time he waited for a ride, but nobody stopped; he felt sure it was because of his clothes. Finally he left the road and went off into the fields to sleep. He ate some bread and a packet of biscuits without feeling hungry, and when he lay down millions of stars mocked at him. They called him "fool" and "idiot" and they taunted him with images of a Jesus whipping along the road in a fast car with a beautiful girl beside him—a blue-eyed blonde. They told him there was still time, that he could begin again and make a success of his life. But his dream held its own, and eventually the stars were silent and the desire for the fast car and the full wallet and the anonymous beauty left him. Slowly he grew peaceful again, and then he slept.

His second crisis had come when he was working for Sanchez Industries. One day at quitting time there came a message. The manager wanted to see him. He had washed up quickly and then waited, feeling nervous and too dirty for the furniture and the rug, in the manager's outer office where the secretary sat. The secretary seemed to share his feelings about himself—she looked at him with distaste and briefly, and did not look at him again when she announced that Señor would see him now. His stomach felt tight with nervousness, but the manager had risen and come around from behind his desk to welcome him, speaking politely and smiling continually. For some time he praised Jesus to himself, praise in which the words "go far" kept recurring. Finally he smiled even more broadly—more broadly, Jesus found himself thinking, than one would believe possible—and offered Jesus the position of personnel manager.

"And that's only the beginning. You're capable and ambitious. You can go far. Take me! The house I was raised in had a dirt floor and my father couldn't read, and look at me now. You're a comer, like me, and the right people have noticed you, just as they noticed me. We're lucky, but we deserve to be lucky. I'm sure you'll do as well as I have. . . ."

Jesus felt his tremor of pleased pride go under and drown in the torrent of words. They had noticed him, all right, but what they had noticed was his ability to help his mates organize a union. They were bribing him to abandon his mates. The manager was still talking; he recalled the fairy tale of the evil-tempered princess whose words emerged from her mouth in the form of lizards and toads.

"Thank you, thank you very much," he said. "But for the moment I'd rather keep my present job."

The stream of toads and lizards had stopped abruptly, but the smile seemed frozen on the manager's face.

"I beg your pardon?" he blurted out, as if he could not possibly have heard aright.

"For the moment I'd like to stay at my present job," said Jesus more firmly.

"I'm afraid you misunderstand me. I am offering you a promotion to managerial rank, a position of responsibility and importance, a move from the workbench into an office, with a commensurate increase in remuneration. . . ." The manager was drowning him in words again, longer and longer ones, as though polysyllables were bound to be persuasive.

"Yes, yes, I understood perfectly. But I have decided not to accept your offer, although I am most grateful for it."

There had been a tense moment of silence. The manager seemed not only astonished but perturbed. Jesus could feel his heart beating so hard that he wondered if the manager could hear it.

"Would you mind telling me why?" asked the manager finally, sounding strained.

The answer came instantly, unhesitantly, as though he had had it ready for a long time: "I belong with my mates, not over them."

The manager stared, then shrugged noncommittally, but when Jesus had left he remained at his desk, feeling pensive and disconcerted. And as he sat his conviction had grown that the young man who had just left was a potential troublemaker and must be got rid of. To have rejected the promotion out of hand like that, without even thinking it over, meant that he was probably a left-wing fanatic. And a left-wing fanatic with managerial ability and a disturbingly forceful personality was trouble incarnate and should be got rid of as quickly as possible. Having so concluded, the manager poured himself a whiskey.

Outside, Jesus had glanced at the clouds, then turned toward home and began walking. He had felt neither righteous nor triumphant, only dismayed and frightened, like a shipwrecked man who sees the rescue craft sailing away from him and cannot cry out to call it back.

In the moonlight Jesus looked at his watch. It was ten past midnight, and he stood up to go to bed. But he paused to listen to the night, and in the silence of the sleeping houses he seemed to hear cries of despair and prayers for help. And the feeling of impotent pain redoubled and returned. "Father," he said aloud into the night, "We count on you. I don't know what I'm doing, and sometimes, like now, I feel very tired. I'm so tired I want to give up. Thy will be done." Then he remembered it was Maundy Thursday night, and he thought of Christ's agony in the garden. He imagined him lying on the ground in the cold light filtering through the olive branches, with his infinite pain breaking out in drops of blood on his forehead. A little way away his friends lay snoring, and their snores, magnified by the silence, magnified his anguish. Christ got up and took a few distracted steps, as if to escape from his pain. In the moonlight his face looked ashen like a corpse's face. He walked to where his friends lay asleep and stood over them for a moment, hesitating, then walked away again. A branch grazed him. He prostrated himself and he cried: "Father, all things are possible to you. Take away this cup from me." He raised his eyes to heaven and saw a bank of clouds cover the face of the moon. Darkness fell on him. He said: "But not my will but yours be done."

Jesus opened his front door, noiselessly so as not to disturb his mother. Remembering Christ had done him good. Whatever his cup might contain, he felt ready to drink it now. His mother heard him come in but said nothing. Let him think she was asleep. And from her soul she prayed: "Lord, help him in whatever is troubling him. You know he's good, he only wants to do what's right. Lord, if anything has to happen to him, let it happen to me instead. I beg you, Lord." Slow, hot tears fell from her eyes.

Jesus lay on his back for a while without thinking, trying to sleep. His sadness was still upon him, but less acute, less focused. He began remembering.

When the neighborhood began to organize, and people began to take notice, the politicians began to arrive. They came up the hill sweating, and the people came out to meet them, wanting to see them, wanting to be touched by powerful officials. The powerful officials wiped their sweating brows, and shook all the hands they could reach, and promised to wipe out poverty. They showed "great interest" and offered "every kind of help" and entreated the people to "count on" them. It was a few months before the elections.

"Count on us."

"The party is with you and we will give you help."

"In December your situation will be radically altered."

"Base organization. An extraordinary example of base organization. That's the way to work."

They had all wanted to talk to Jesus.

One of them was more explicit than any of the others. "You are a born leader. You can mobilize the people better than any theoretician. If you wanted...." The politician had stopped speaking to read Jesus' face, but it told him nothing and Jesus said nothing. The politician had looked around longingly for some shade, but there was none and he went on: "You understand, we can't talk properly here. We need some peace and quiet to discuss things, because I think you and I have a lot to discuss. You could go far in politics." He gave Jesus a meaningful look. "Why don't you come and talk to us some day?"

The politician's white hand had slipped a card with the address of party headquarters on it into Jesus' dark hand.

And then the politicians had gone back down the hill in the dust, bestowing smiles right and left.

"This is our chance," said Pedro when the politicians had gone. "You will go, won't you?"

Jesus shrugged. He seemed to be looking inward, listening to his own feelings.

"You could get on the council, and go from there to congress. People listen to you. All you need is the chance to talk to them. Christ! You might even be president one day! Who knows?"

Pedro's visionary eyes made his dark face look even fiercer.

In his mind's eye Jesus was seeing his name in all the headlines, hearing it chanted by spellbound crowds. It would be the realization of his dreams—power to transform the world. He felt giddy with possibilities, mad with hope, possessed by the prospect of power. Then he shook his head.

"Our political parties stink, Pedro my friend. They talk 'the good of people' but they mean 'winning the next election.' They don't care about the people, they don't know about the people, and they don't want to know. Do you think they show up here before every election because they love us? Because suddenly they've seen the light and they want justice? We're votes, man—poor, dirty, smelly votes, but votes. That's all they come for, and at that they can't wait to leave and go back where they belong—to the air conditioning and the ice cubes in the glasses with the good whiskey. They can't give us justice without giving up their air conditioning and their ice cubes, and they know it, so don't hold your breath waiting for justice from the politicians. When they offer us a crumb of power, it's only to divide us and confuse us and sidetrack us. Pedro, beware of politicians offering power to the people!"

Pedro frowned. He was beginning to feel impatient. "You are a dreamer. You throw away all your best chances. You're all visions and no strategy. How are you going to change anything if you despise politics?"

"Politicizing, Pedro. I'm interested in politicizing, not politics," said Jesus. "Politics won't get us anywhere, but politicizing will."

Pedro looked at him. "What's the difference?"

"Politics is other people promising to give us justice, so

we'll vote for them, and breaking their promises after they're elected. Politicizing means us organizing ourselves till we're strong enough to get justice for ourselves. It's very slow, but it's the only way that works, at least for now. The rest is all lies."

Pedro's mouth felt dry and dusty. The sun seemed hotter. "Bah," he said finally, "you play with words. Power is power, once you've got it, and you could use it for everyone's good if you weren't so goddam finicky."

Jesus did not answer. Still frowning, Pedro went away.

"I heard you talking to Pedro," said Simon, appearing suddenly as if he had sprung out of the ground. "I fully agree with you. All politicians are opportunist shit. Especially this can of bourgeois worms babbling about justice for us when they mean power for themselves. They deceive the people and delay the revolution. What we have to do is sharpen the contradictions, arm the people, and fight for victory. Only bloodshed will solve the contradictions in society, but we shall win because we are the majority."

Simon paused, looking into Jesus' face for signs of agreement, and Jesus looked back at him but did not agree. Everyone in the neighborhood knew that Simon belonged to the Red Flag. Jesus valued him highly.

"Your impatience is killing you, Simon," said Jesus. "Can't you see that conditions aren't ripe for your revolution? Don't you realize that your violence and terrorism just play into the hands of the authorities? Without you people as an excuse it might be harder for the government to justify repression and counter-terror. Simon, stop listening so much to the voice of your revolutionary theories, and try to hear the voices of our people. They're milder than your theories—and more realistic."

Simon glared at him in a fury of impatience. "It's not impatience that's killing me! It's oppression! How long are we supposed to be patient? And why is it more realistic to wait than to fight now?"

It was a cry from the heart, and Jesus heard it and understood. "Yes," he said. "Injustice is intolerable, absolutely. It is the root of inhumanity. But fighting just for the sake of doing something may not accomplish anything. All that blood you keep wanting to shed—it may not weed out injustice, it may fertilize it. We have to be careful about our methods."

"The people will fight if you tell them to."

Jesus interrupted him with a look.

"Are you by any chance suggesting that I lead the people to a bloody self-sacrifice?"

"It's better to die like men than live like slaves."

"But those aren't the only two alternatives. What's the point of dying heroically if with a little thought and patience we could learn to live decently?"

Simon was silent for a long moment. "I wish you luck," he said finally.

"We'll succeed together. That's the key."

Jesus turned over in bed, feeling sleepy at last. Outside a cock crowed, although it was not yet two o'clock. He felt calm, purged of sadness. He was glad he had chosen this life and stayed with it. Probably he would suffer for it, and probably he would not see justice accomplished, but so be it. It would be enough to know that he spent his life working for it. He had chosen the task, and that was all a person could do. The outcome was in God's hands.

He closed his eyes and slept, with something like a smile on his lips.

GOOD FRIDAY

XIII

Señora REMEDIOS WAS GOING HOME, walking down the hill via the concrete steps. She walked slowly and ponderously, resting her weight for an instant on each step, as fat people do. The dull roar of the city below came up the hill to meet her. The water in the drainage ditch smelled foul. Señora Remedios was hot and tired and irritated at Gramoven. The walls made of cardboard, the women always pregnant, the kids naked, the men jobless and shiftless, with no money except for rum and no initiative except for making more kids. The kids that they made grew up like rabbits—on their own almost as soon as they could walk, begging, stealing, shining shoes, selling newspapers. Scrounging. In that neighborhood fathers weren't providers—they weren't even fathers. She nearly had a heart attack every week climbing these stairs to give catechism classes, and the kids didn't even come; the parents didn't bother sending them. Hopeless good-for-nothing—no education, no religion—a bunch of animals! And now to top everything they had all gone haywire over that Jesus, a godless communist infiltrator, a menace to order and religion.

Señora Remedios had progressed from irritation to fury. At this moment she hated all of Gramoven.

She continued on her way to the dirt track that was the last stop on the bus route. She had to get home quickly to keep her promise to the Mater Dolorosa—she had done it for thirty years—to go on procession to "the seven churches." There was no bus at the stop, but Judas' combination store and bar

99

was open, and she could see Judas inside, leaning his elbows on the counter and deep in thought. Señora Remedios realized she was thirsty.

"Bring me something cold, Judas. I need cooling off."

He set a glass down before her and agreed perfunctorily that it was very hot.

Señora Remedios began to drink and to sweat copiously. "It's a long time since I've seen Jesus," she said.

Judas shrugged. He opened his mouth but closed it again without speaking.

"He's been fired again," Señora Remedios offered.

"Yes, I heard."

Señora Remedios took another long drink. "And he'll be fired from every job, till there's nobody left who'll hire him. Especially now that they're about to find out what he really is."

"Look, I've got nothing to do with this Jesus. I don't know why you're telling me all this."

Señora Remedios tried again to look him in the eyes.

"Really?" she said coyly. "I thought you were one of his most faithful followers."

Now Judas was really angry. He grabbed the empty glass and shouted with his back turned, "Maybe I was once. But I have nothing to do with him now. Have you got that straight?"

He turned to look at her. Señora Remedios was smiling at him maliciously. Finally this fish was interested in her bait! "Oh, so you've heard he was mixed up in the kidnapping of those brothers," she said evenly.

Judas actually recoiled and turned pale. That would teach him to try and act cool with her!

"What?" he said, and his voice was shaking.

Señora Remedios shrugged. She flicked her tongue over her lips. "Don't play village idiot with me, Judas. You must know about it. Everyone around here knows."

The bus had arrived. She dropped a coin on the counter and went out to it, savoring his discomfiture.

Judas watched her heave herself on, pay, wait for her change, and sit down in one of the front seats. As the bus pulled away she smiled at him flirtatiously and waved. Automatically, he waved back raising the hand that still held her coin between finger and thumb.

Then the bus was gone and the dust was settling, and with no customers in the shop he had nothing to do but agonize over what that tub of lard had said. Could it be true? A guerrilla? A terrorist? Was that why Jesus made him so profoundly uncomfortable? Had he, Judas, been sensing the communist wolf under the Christly mask? If that woman was telling the truth then he, Judas, had sinned by working with him, by ignoring his own intuition and Father Sanchez's advice. He couldn't leave things like that. He had to pay for his sin. He must uproot the evil before it was too late. He must hand over Jesus.

He stood petrified at where his thoughts had led him. He shook his head as if that would rid him of the idea. "No, it can't be so," he told himself. "It must be just old women's gossip and spite. I have no proofs. I can't do it. No, no, no, I can't do it."

He breathed deeply, but he could not calm down. His skin burned as if with fever, and doubts racketed through his head. What if lard-tub had been telling the truth? What if his silence were contributing to the triumph of evil? Hadn't he sworn to Father Sanchez to be a true soldier of Christ?

Judas felt screams bursting inside him. Outside he could see real things and people in the ordinary daylight, but he had nothing to do with them. He was shut up in his own torment and ordinary things had no power to reassure him. His heart was hammering painfully.

"Hello, Judas, how are you?" It was the standard greeting, stale with use, but Madalena always sounded as though she meant every word. How he felt was one of the last things Judas wanted to tell anyone, and Madalena was one of the last people he wanted to tell it to.

"Hello," he replied brusquely, not looking at her.

"Listen, Judas, I need a few things. I've invited Jesus and a few friends to supper tonight, and I want you to come too. Will you?"

"Can't, I'm sorry," he said, busily piling up some cans of cold drinks. "I'm busy tonight."

"Please come, Judas. It's not that often I can afford to have friends in for dinner, and the group isn't complete without you."

Madalena's voice was warm and coaxing. Like all the women in Gramoven she was prematurely aged, but unlike most of them she was still beautiful. In spite of himself he answered her gently.

"I'll try my best, but I can't promise. There is something else I said I'd do."

Something was bothering him terribly, she knew, and she wished he would tell her what it was.

"I'd be so pleased if you came," she said. "And so would Jesus."

She hesitated a moment and went on: "Last night I saw him thinking. All alone outside. He was sad." She wanted to add, "Like you," but didn't dare. So she only ventured: "Is anything the matter, Judas?"

He wanted to tell her. He wanted her to heal his doubts and end his pain.

"No, nothing, why?"

"You look miserable, Judas. You look as though you want to cry."

Judas sighed. "It's so hard to be faithful to Christ," was all he said, but Madalena suddenly felt afraid. Something terrible was going to happen to Judas, and somehow it would involve Jesus.

"What do you mean?"

Judas shrugged. "I don't know. It gets more and more confusing. You don't know what or who to believe. Everyone's truth is someone else's lie. You think you have a dream and it turns into a nightmare."

He was looking at her now, with such bewilderment and bitterness that she felt even greater fear.

"Don't talk like that, Judas. Truth is truth. Jesus' dream is no nightmare. You can believe in Jesus."

"I only believe in Christ," cried Judas. "People are all liars and hypocrites. What proof do we have that Jesus is any different?"

"We all believe in Christ too, and Jesus believes more than anyone."

Judas glared at her. "Do you think he really believes?"

"Of course, Judas. What's the matter with you? Do you think he could love people the way he does if he didn't love God?"

"Then why? . . ." Judas shook his head. His question trailed away. He looked shrunken, like an old man.

"I know what some people say about him, but I also know it's not true. Judas, all you have to do is think about Jesus and then think about goodness and you'll know that Jesus is good."

For the first time that afternoon Judas smiled. She was so childlike in her passionate defense of Jesus and so maternal in her concern for his misery. Judas was touched, but his doubts were not appeased.

"Well, what is it you need for tonight?" he asked, briskly changing the subject.

XIV

"BABY, WOULD YOU RUN TO THE STORE and get me a small can of oil and half a kilo of sugar that I forgot?"

The child left off kneading the corn cakes and went to wash her hands. She took the money her mother held out to her and smiled. Her eyes were very dark. "Like her father's," thought Madalena, "but clearer."

"You can buy yourself an ice and one for Ramoncito."

"Don't you want one, mum?"

Madalena looked away. "No, I don't feel like an ice today. And hurry. I'm going to need the oil very soon."

The girl went out into the sun, and Madalena paused in her work to look lovingly after her from the door. She saw her go down the dirt track, jump the ditch full of dirty water, and disappear in the direction of the shop. She walked like a young girl beginning to grow up. Madalena turned back to her cooking. The teacher had told her Mariella was a fine student, and she treasured the knowledge. She had only to think about it to feel content. "I hope she doesn't have to go through what I've been through," she thought, and the memory of her past crowded out her contentment in her child.

She saw Mariella's father's eyes again. Just the eyes—dark, compelling, and sweet—she could not remember his face. She had been fourteen years old when those eyes first looked at her, and made her heart leap, and kindled fires in her flesh. Those eyes had been the beginning of Mariella, but they had never seen her. He had gone away without even knowing that the girl who had loved him on the river bank was carrying his baby.

She moved to Cumana when Mariella was barely two. She found work as a servant. They paid her four bolivars a day and her meals. She was happy.

Happy until the master began to look at her too much, staring at her legs and breasts whenever his wife was out of the room. She avoided him as much as she could, but one day he told her she was too pretty to sleep alone, and not long after that came the afternoon when the children were, as usual, at school and the mistress had gone to the hairdresser to have the blond streaks put in her hair—an all-day affair— and suddenly there was the master. His face was stupid with lust, and he babbled of wanting her and divorcing his wife. He was heavy and clumsy and he grunted as he was hurting her.

When she began to show, they dismissed her.

When Ramoncito was born, it was a while before she loved him, because he looked like his father.

She couldn't find work in Cumana and finally, in desperation, she went to see the master in his office. He owed it to her and her children to help her, she told herself angrily.

He gave her fare-money to Caracas, and a letter of introduction to a "high-class restaurant that needed pretty girls as waitresses"—that turned out to be a brothel. She wore a bikini and served drinks and was "agreeable to the clients in every way."

Juancito's crying broke into her train of thought. Madalena went into the bedroom, which was divided from the living room by sheets of cardboard. The child was awake and hungry. She made up a bottle, and Juancito sucked at it with his eyes closed till it was almost empty and he fell asleep again. Madalena took the nipple from his mouth and kissed him. Then Ramoncito stirred in his sleep beside him, and she kissed him too.

She learned to be "agreeable to the clients," and she learned to anesthetize herself—to close off her mind from her work. Her employers were satisfied and her children were fed. She never complained. But when the important-looking person took a small whip out of his attaché case and told her she must beat him she did not understand. At first she thought he was going to beat her and was terribly frightened, but not nearly so terrified as when she understood him correctly. For a moment she could only think that he was mad; then it occurred to her that it was a trap—that she would take the whip and then he would kill her and say he had done it in self-defense. She had heard of such things.

"Take this and beat me. As hard as you can."

He put the whip into her nerveless hand and knelt beside the bed, biting the pillow against the anticipated pain. His back was tanned and smelled of sun cream. Madalena felt her strength fail her. She screamed and ran out of the room.

She was fired again.

She wandered the streets for a few days looking for work. Caracas seemed enormous and hostile; the streets were full of cars and empty of people. She couldn't read, and a shoe-shine boy charged her two bolivars to read the want ads in the evening papers.

She began working as a waitress in the Mexico Bar.

Her fifth day there she met Carlos, and they had half a bottle of *cacique* together when her shift was over. Then they went to his room. Carlos began coming every night. He wouldn't be served by anybody else. And when he couldn't come to the bar he phoned her there. He said he cared about her and he wanted to take care of her and make her happy.

In the end she believed him and moved in with him. Carlos worked as a janitor in a college. He was a rough man but kind to her. He gave her money to feed the children, and she liked him in bed.

The day Carlos lost his job because a student's mother complained about him, he took out all his fury at life on Madalena. He beat her with his fists and the broomstick. He cursed, yelling like a madman, as he beat her. He was beating life itself for treating him so hard. Mariella grabbed his leg and hung on, crying with terror and screaming at him to stop beating her mother. To be interfered with by a child who wasn't even his own maddened Carlos even more. He struck Mariella so hard that she fell to the floor, and then Madalena went for him with the scissors. Neighbors broke up the fight.

Madalena moved out. She took the children back to the woman who had boarded them while she worked in the brothel, and she got a job in another bar. For extra money she went with men. There was very little now that frightened her or disgusted her, although the time a drunk vomited on her she nearly killed him. She barely remembered the dark-eyed boy who had fathered Mariella, and she never thought about the dreaming girl who had given herself to him on the river bank. Sometimes she thought vaguely about dear God and Our Lady, who were supposed to love everyone.

She had to move to Gramoven when urban renewal demolished San Agustin. It was in the neighborhood school that she met Jesus. She had heard that grown-ups met there evenings to study and discuss neighborhood problems. Out of loneliness one day when she was not working she plucked up the courage to go. Jesus welcomed her and introduced her to the others. He seemed to be an educated person, even though he lived in the neighborhood like all the others. He spoke in simple words that everybody understood, and he was very kind. When he looked at her she remembered her former self and her present life seemed a weariness and a thing of revulsion.

She came back every chance she got and went out of her way to speak to him, and at work she thought constantly of his words and his eyes. Even with other men she thought about him. It never occurred to her that she was falling in love — anymore than she thought of it as "turning over a new leaf"—but one day she stopped going with men.

"Here's your shopping, mum, and the money. Mr. Judas wouldn't charge me anything. He said it was his contribution to tonight's supper."

Mariella was flushed and happy. The walk up the hill had given her a healthy color and made her prettier.

"Mr. Judas is very good, isn't he, mum?"

"Yes. He's coming to eat with us tonight."

"Ramoncito is still asleep. What shall I do with the ice, mum? It'll melt in this heat."

"Eat it yourself, child, but don't tell him about it when he wakes up or he'll have a fit."

"Don't you want it, mum? I ate mine walking up the hill."

"No, child, eat it yourself."

Mariella hesitated a moment. "Better if I wake up Ramoncito and give it to him. He's slept long enough, and it'll be a nice way to wake up."

XV

MADALENA BEGAN WASHING UP. She was happy. They had all eaten heartily, and Jesus had told her that everything was delicious. Kind as he was, he never lied, and she felt pleased and triumphant and absurdly joyful that she had been able to do something for him, even if it was only to cook him a good dinner.

"I'll help you wash up," she heard Jesus say beside her.

"No, please, that's not man's work."

"Stop repeating the nonsense you hear. Why must washing up always be women's work and never men's? It's not right that you should spend the whole afternoon cooking and serving and we shouldn't even give you a hand with the cleaning up."

"No, Jesus, not necessary. Mariella will help me. She's a big girl now and helps me a lot."

"Well, today let her play with her brothers or rest. I want to help you."

Jesus took the dish towel from the child and began drying plates. Mariella stood there, saying nothing, watching him. Madalena too said nothing. She felt she had never in her whole life been so happy as she was at this moment with Jesus beside her.

"You're my guest—and you're an educated man—and you stand here drying my dishes! You're not supposed to," she said at last in a voice that trembled slightly.

Jesus emptied the dirty water from the wash basin and poured in fresh water from the bucket. "But I *am* supposed to. It's such a stupid lie that some people are better than others and entitled to be waited on! And yet everyone keeps on believing it. Even you believe it. Madalena, there is no such thing as more important and less important. We are all different, we are all equal, we should all help each other. If everyone believed that, it's all it would take to change the world. Don't you see?"

They continued washing and drying in silence. Madalena was wishing she had a thousand dishes to wash so that she could stay there forever, in silence, very close to Jesus.

"How's work?" she heard Jesus ask presently.

"O.K. It's going well. Only, the pay is terrible in that factory. Three hundred a month. Hardly enough to make ends meet." She paused and then, still busily washing up, not looking at him, she went on. "Look, I've been thinking. You've been fired again. If you have trouble finding another job, you know you and your mother can always come and eat with me."

For a moment Jesus was too moved to reply. Then: "Thank you, Madalena, thank you. You are so good."

The washing-up stopped abruptly. Madalena glanced at Jesus and shook her head sadly. "Don't say I'm good. If you only knew. . . . You mightn't even want to be here."

Jesus smiled. "I do know, and I am here. You are good and you always have been. If men took advantage of you, because you were young and poor and powerless, that makes them evil, not you."

If she tried to speak aloud, she knew, she would burst into tears.

"Thank you," she whispered.

In the next room their friends were arguing.

"What you want is to stir up class warfare. As a Christian I could never go along with that." Judas's voice was harsh.

"Christian? You're a collaborator, not a Christian! Altar boy to our oppressors, that's what you are. It's people like you who make liberation impossible. Our priests are hand in glove with the rich, but as long as the enemy wears a cassock you're his faithful follower, his most obedient pupil, his willing cat's-paw. Marx knew what he was talking about: Religion certainly is the opiate of the people."

Simon raised his coffee cup to conceal the triumphant smile he couldn't control. He was pleased with his speech and with himself.

"That doesn't mean that all religion is the opiate of the people," said Juan. "Christianity, properly understood and really lived, is dynamite, not opium. Che himself said that when Christians realized the true implications of their faith there would be no stopping the revolution in Latin America."

Simon looked at Juan admiringly. The boy always went straight to the heart of issues, and without ever raising his voice. He was the best thinker among them, apart from Jesus.

"That's quite true," said Pedro. "Judas's trouble is he's afraid. Just say the word 'revolution' or 'struggle' and he thinks about maybe getting hurt, so he hides behind religion. Angels in white robes aren't going to bring justice down from the clouds! Good Christians are ready to fight for what's right—like me!"

Judas looked at him with hatred. "You've always been a flag-waver. And a fake. Lots of hot air, but when the chips are down no one can ever find you."

"Are you calling me a coward, you pious fart, you shitty shop-keeper?"

"Easy, easy," said Jesus as he came in. "Very friendly conversation you're having, aren't you? Can't you show some respect in Madalena's house? I thought good food made people feel relaxed and agreeable! Besides, if we can't stay friends, how are we going to unite others?"

"They started fighting about words," said Felipe. "As if words could fix what's wrong with the world."

"They get like fighting cocks," added Tomas.

"I was just envying Judas's bravery," said Pedro jeeringly. "Want to see a human chameleon? Just say 'class struggle' and watch him turn yellow!"

Judas looked sick with hatred.

Jesus sat down between them.

"What is the point of talking like this, Pedro? Do you learn anything about the other person's point of view? Do you convince him of yours? The most useful part of discussing is listening for what's right and true in what the other person says. It doesn't sound as if you do much listening."

"I listen to what's worth hearing. There's not much worth hearing when Judas opens his mouth."

"You're an amazing man, Pedro. I never knew one man could be so right about so many things," said Jesus dryly. "Seriously, friend, we all have something to teach and a lot to learn. That's why we must listen to one another. We should talk not to wound each other but to learn from each other, because so far we know very little."

There was silence. Judas and Pedro did not look at Jesus or at each other. Their eyes were fixed on the table.

"And you, Judas, you shouldn't let words frighten you. Look at the realities and don't get bogged down in words. The world really is divided by classes. There is the class of those who make decisions, give orders, have everything, oppress others. . . . Then there's us, who have no voice, no wordly goods, no decent jobs, no say in our own lives—nothing. We're the oppressed and they're the ruling class, Judas, and they'll do everything in their power to keep it that way, because their luxuries come out of our misery. Refusing to see it doesn't make it not so. The class struggle is their doing, though they refuse to see that they started it by the way they live. That's why we must unite, learn solidarity, and oppose them—not to change places with them but to create a world where no one has too little because someone else has too much."

Tomas took up the argument: "It's obvious, what Jesus says. It's clearer than water. Yesterday I saw Santiago in Ojo de Agua. He and his kids were picking through garbage, fighting the buzzards for it. It stank like hell, but there they were. They don't love the smell of garbage any better than the rich do, but they need the eight bolivars a ton they get for the waste paper they collect. When some people have to live off what others throw away, what would you call that, Judas?

A truly Christian world? Do you think Santiago pokes around in garbage for a living because he loves garbage? Do you think I work in a cotton mill because I like coughing my lungs out? Do you think it's me and my mates who demand three-month contracts? Hell, the bosses write those contracts to make sure we can't ever form a union, and it's sign them or starve. Do you think Jesus keeps getting laid off because he gets a thrill out of being fired? Or because he loves going hungry? Christ, Judas, all these things are *done to us* by the rich! Wouldn't you call that class oppression? What's Christian about it?"

"No, I tell you, I've never said it was Christian," said Judas, panting as if he had been running. "Have I ever said so? Of course I don't think it's right. I only say that it's not right to fight injustice with hate and violence. I am a Christian, and I know I am commanded to love my neighbors, including the unjust ones."

Pedro said nothing. He only made a gesture of disgust to show it was useless to go on talking to Judas.

"I agree with you, Judas," said Jesus. "I also believe that our first duty is to love others. But love is a dynamic, fighting, active thing. Love in the oppressed should become a force for liberation. That's why Christ, who told his disciples to love, also told them to expect persecution, prison, and death. He knew that love as he meant it would be intolerable to those who live by hate and greed."

"But he also commanded us to love our enemies!" Judas exploded.

"Right," answered Jesus. "He commanded us to love our enemies, meaning that we would have enemies. People who treat us like dirt are not our friends! He told us to love our enemies, but he did not say we wouldn't have any, or that we shouldn't fight them. The Christian must love everybody, but not everybody in the same way. We must love the oppressed by fighting on their side for their liberation. We must love the oppressors by fighting them head on, so that they too have the chance to become human, because nobody can be human who oppresses others in any way. That's why Christian love must oppose and struggle against every kind of injustice, every trampling on the rights of others. That's why Christian love, rightly understood, is such a powerful weapon. It's the most powerful weapon of all. Much stronger than hatred. Hatred aims to destroy and smash; it produces nothing new. Love wants to build a human world for everybody—including even the former oppressors."

The loving admiration in Juan's eyes was matched by the glittering anger in Judas's.

"You're a real artist of double-talk," said Judas. "I can't talk like you but at least I think straight. I know what you are saying can't be Christian. And anyway, where do you get the authority to preach about Christian love to us? I'll stick with what I'm taught by priests, who have studied it properly."

Jesus looked at him sadly.

"Christianity isn't in books, Judas, but in human hearts. To be a Christian you don't need to study a lot, but to love."

"Yes, love, but not your kind of love! I want no part of your kind of love," Judas shouted. A vein was swelling in his forehead. "Love is a weapon, love is fighting, love is struggle. Love is hate—right, Jesus? No, thank you. It took me a while to see through you, but from now on you can take your love and all the rest of your ideas and peddle them somewhere else!"

He had gotten to his feet during this tirade, and now he stormed out, swinging around in the doorway to glare at them all for a second. Pedro watched him go with a derisive smile. Tomas and Felipe lowered their eyes. Jesus looked profoundly troubled but said nothing.

It was Juan's voice that broke the silence, calling after Judas:

"Don't go, Judas. Come back. Calm down. Try and listen to what Jesus wants to say without getting so agitated."

Judas did not go back.

It had grown dark during the quarrel, and the thin slice of moon that had risen gave little light. His heart was pounding. He strode through the darkness like a man sure of his destination and impatient to get there, but he had no idea where he was going and no set purpose but to get as far away from Jesus as possible.

"He was always a coward," said Pedro.

"No, Pedro, cowards never go against the tide," answered Jesus. "He is a soul in torment trying to see the light. He needs all the help we can give him."

They were all looking at him now. Juan's eyes were sad. Madalena's were full of love—and fear.

XVI

*T*HE SOLDIER WAITED FOR THE OTHER TWO CONVICTS TO PASS *and looked at the one they called Christ. He was no longer carrying the cross. A sturdy farmer had been conscripted to carry it for him, or he might not have reached the top alive. The last time he had fallen he had lain motionless on the ground beneath the cross-beam. It would have been cheating the law to nail him up already a corpse. Where was the punishment in that? And where the lesson for this stinking pack of malcontents and subversives?*

Christ's face was sickly green and bloody. He stumbled like a drunkard amid shouts and blows. The people jostling him were excited, like animals in heat. Their eyes glittered and stared. There were always a lot of babies made after a public execution. Queer, but there it was. The soldier stood to let the man with the cross go by. He was coarse-featured and angry-looking and very strong; he shouldered his burden effortlessly. At the top he set the cross down beside the hole, shrugged his shoulders, and headed back downhill without looking at anyone. Apparently he did not want to stay for the fun.

When the Christ reached him, the soldier grabbed his arm. The condemned man turned very slowly and looked at him with great pain but without hatred or fear. His face was filthy with spittle and blood and his eyes were sunken and dark but peaceful. The soldier let go of his arm. "They say he is mad, but his eyes are sane," he thought. "Perhaps after so much pain he doesn't know what's happening."

Simon the Zealot mingled with the crowd, fingering the dagger concealed under his shirt and watching in an agony of helplessness.

They undressed him roughly. Pieces of skin came away with his clothes. He stood naked before them, covered with wounds in which the fresh blood glistened. Someone beside Simon made a coarse joke, but very few people laughed and the laughter had fear in it. Simon did not look at them. Behind Christ there was a sudden sound of hammering and a great wail. Then there was more hammering and strangled cries. Simon thought they must have stuffed a cloth in the criminal's mouth to muffle his cries. He did not look. He knew that the one they were hammering up now was Dismas, a Zealot like himself, a Roman-hater. Soon he would no longer be able to hate anyone.

. . . unless there was a miracle. Christ had promised one when they were vainly urging him to lead an uprising against Rome. He had answered—not once but often—that his death was necessary to establish his kingdom. And that once he was dead he would return in power and majesty with legions of victorious angels. Simon looked skyward and saw storm clouds gathering on the horizons, and he felt a pulse of hope. The second convict had been nailed up. The air rang with screams and curses, now they were laying out Jesus on the cross. He spotted John and the two women, Jesus' mother and Mary Magdalene, behind a little knot of staunch friends who were offering Jesus poppy-juice to lessen the pain. Simon admired their courage—they were marked men, all of them, in Roman eyes—but he was glad not to be one of them. Jesus' mother was leaning lightly on John's shoulder. She was not crying, but Mary Magdalene was. Noiselessly, with tears running down her chalk-white face. John was staring at the ground. He was not afraid to stand openly among all these people as the condemned man's friend, but he could not watch what was about to happen. He was only a boy, after all. Probably this was his first crucifixion. Certainly he didn't seem the sort who went for amusement. Again the staccato sound of the hammer *and the lingering, hoarse scream. Simon dug his nails into his palms and felt his bowels loosen. He stared at the sky again lest someone see and note the anguish in his face. The clouds were thicker now, and darker.*

"If they don't die soon, we'll be caught in a storm."

"Yes," said Simon, still looking at the sky. "Those first two will last quite a while," continued the voice, "but that last one will go soon. He's already half dead from the beating. They say that the soldiers roughed him up afterwards on their own. They must have. Look at the crown of thorns. And his face is all swollen and black and blue. That's from fists, when the commander isn't looking."

The man wanted conversation, but Simon did not reply. They were raising the cross now. The crowd seethed. People screamed. The cross lurched and shuddered into its hole, and the crucified man groaned terribly. The massing clouds had not yet reached the hilltop, and the sun was bright and hot on his face.

Four soldiers held the cross upright while others filled the hole with stones and earth and stamped them firm. Their work was done then, and they began to clean their hammers.

Simon ventured to look at the middle cross. Jesus' lips moved as if he were praying. Simon remembered how these same lips had taught them to pray, to rid their hearts of weariness and anger. They seemed to be praying still, but it would not be for long. Unless there was a miracle, it could not be for long.

The crowd seemed to be getting bored. They had climbed the hill in all that heat for a better spectacle, a greater struggle against death, sharper cries. Some had even hoped that he would use one of his tricks to confound the Romans at the last minute. But nothing. One scream and a few groans. It wasn't much of a show. A trickle of people was already headed back down the hill for a drink and the relative coolness of home or tavern.

"Hey, you! You said you would destroy the Temple and raise it again in three days! What have you got to say now? You saved others, but you can't save yourself. Come down

from the cross and we'll believe in you." It was a loud voice, full of hatred, and it carried over the crowd.

Others took up the taunt: "Come down from the cross! Come down from the cross!"

People laughed, and craned to see the faces of the speakers.

The man on the middle cross opened his eyes. He was no longer praying. He looked at all the people without moving his head. Simon could hear his breath beginning to whistle. He straightened himself, thrusting his weight against the nails through his wrists in order to take in enough air to speak, and cried out, clearly and audibly: "Father, forgive them. They don't know what they are doing."

The taunts died away. The crowd stood still. After a moment, here and there, someone tried to laugh.

The crucified man repeated his prayer, but this time his voice sounded strangled and the words were slurred: "Father, forgive them. They don't know what they are doing."

Simon felt transfixed by the cry as by a spear. He saw that the centurion, who had been dicing with his men to pass the time till the criminals should die, was standing up now and looking with interest into the crucified man's face. As he watched, John went forward and spoke with the centurion, then returned and helped Jesus' mother to the foot of the cross. She raised her head to look at her son, and the shadow of the cross fell on her face. Still she did not weep, but she was white as one who had bled to death.

"He is dying without anger, forgiving, dying like a saint," Simon heard a woman say behind him. "This man must be one of God's great prophets."

Simon did not turn round but he guessed that the woman was crying. A cloud covered the sun and was instantly pierced by the sun again. Jerusalem below panted with heat and dust. His dreams were about to die, there on that cross. They'd have to go on waiting, for who knew how many years more, for redemption from Rome and from shame. Simon reread the words on the cross: "Jesus of Nazareth, King of the Jews." The ghost of a smile twitched at his lips: This was Roman obtuseness at its most thick-headed. What kind of king disclaimed power, declined command, refused subjects? Only one who wore a crown of thorns and died on the cross. There would be no miracle. He would die very soon, and he would return to his home in Roman Jerusalem. It would be the better part of valor not to look for the others. Anyway, all of them except John had fled and were even now on their way back to their villages in Galilee. They would go back to their fishing nets dreaming on the lake, remembering dreams. For himself, he would try to become more active in the Party. They would organize better so that one day all the people would follow them. And on that day the Romans would flee in panic, terrified by the power of Yahweh in the person of the Jews. He had been mistaken to follow the Nazarene. The Nazarene was dying, suffocating, deserted, almost alone. Unless, as he had said, by his death. . . . Hadn't he often shown Godlike powers? Simon realized suddenly that he was still hoping.

He looked at the sky again and then at the crucified man. He was speaking to his mother and John. Simon couldn't hear him. Mary Magdalene was looking at him with eyes blazing with love, and Simon envied the woman's courage. "He took her out of her evil life and gave her a heart as brave as Ruth's. She is braver than any of us men. A woman like her will one day give birth to the Messiah."

A legion of clouds attacked the sun and conquered it. Darkness fell on them and the heat dropped. People looked up at the sky.

"It'll rain soon. Storm coming."

"Yes, with all that heat it was bound to come. It'll be thundering soon."

The trickle of people heading down the hill swelled rapidly.

There was a great crash of thunder. The crucified men seemed to be talking to each other. Then Dismas began shouting, cursing the crowd and the Romans and his wounds like a madman. The other one was quiet. He seemed to be looking fixedly at Jesus.

Jesus' breathing grew more labored. Blood trickled in slow drops from the nails. It ran down the wood and stained the ground. Great flies buzzed around the stains.

"I'm thirsty."

He spoke as if he were already in the delirium of death. One of the soldiers looked doubtfully at the centurion, who nodded. The soldier held up a sponge to him on the end of his lance. He pressed the sponge to Jesus' lips and dark liquid flowed from it.

"Yes, he's dying now. He can barely breathe," said a man beside Simon. "Any minute now. . . . I don't know why they killed him. He was surely a good man. He only did good, and this is how he ends." He was a small, dark man with an enormous hooked nose, and he looked sad.

"Yes, soon everything will be over," Simon replied, and his voice revealed for the first time the ache in his heart.

The small man looked at him curiously. "Were you one of his disciples?" he asked, his enormous nose coming closer.

Simon shrugged. "I knew him. I liked him," he said and changed the subject. "There'll be a storm soon."

The small man sniffed the sky with his great nose. "I don't know," he said doubtfully. "Sometimes the sky is full of rain and not a drop of rain falls. Just flashes and thunder. If the wind rises the clouds will blow over."

Jesus gave an unintelligible cry. His lips moved soundlessly and then stopped, half open.

"He must have died," said the small man. Simon stared at the sky.

"That woman over there is his mother. Poor thing."

XVII

CRAZY MARRERO WAS ANGRY AT THE NIGHT. He looked at it for a while, trying to burn it away with his look, then spoke a few voiceless words, shaking his head. He picked up a handful of dust and clutched it, then, with a cry, threw it into the night's eyes to blind it. His cry shivered through the houses and died away in the unresponsive night. Finally the madman sat down on the ground, squeezing his head between his bony hands as though throttling the thoughts that tormented him.

"We kill him," he said aloud. "We kill him every time he is born again. He keeps being born again, and we keep killing him. Our hands are blood-stained, and every time the blood begins to dry we steep them in fresh blood. Christ's blood." He was shouting now. "You, all of you pretending to be asleep, look at your hands and you'll see they are bloody. He didn't die in Jerusalem once and for all, much as we want to think so. It's here every day that we keep killing him."

Crazy Marrero was silent, and the silence seemed total. The roar of the city had quieted, the sky was empty of stars, and the wind seemed to have wearied and gone to rest somewhere far away. The madman communed with himself, then drew a deep breath and cried: "We all have blood on our hands. You no-good, rutting, swilling men! You fill yourselves with beer and rum and your women with babies and then you abandon them. You make whores of your women and orphans of your children, and then disease kills them, or hunger, or drugs, or the police. Their blood is on your hands and it is Christ's blood. Look at your hands! It is not just my madness speaking. Look at your hands, and you'll see the blood. My words are the voices of the women you whored and the children you begot and murdered. The cries of your children reach the stars, and the stars cannot bear it and block their ears with clouds to escape those cries. Come outside and look! The stars are all behind the clouds! And you women are no better: taking one drunk after another into your dirty beds while the children you already have roam like dogs among the garbage and grow up good for nothing except doing nothing and getting high and listening to Yankee music played full blast on stolen radios! Drunken pigs, whores, junkies, girls who flaunt themselves in bars till the men go crazy and the knives come out! You all have blood on your hands. You are murdering Christ."

Crazy Marrero stopped to think again. He continued more quietly.

"But no. Not everybody who hears me has blood on his hands. Not Jesus, nor Maria, his mother. Not Madalena either. She saw good and recognized it and followed it even though her whole life had been evil. Those are the only ones with no blood on their hands. Only three among so many. All the rest of us have blood on our hands, some a little, some a lot."

Crazy Marrero sat down again. His eyes were calmer and his frenzy seemed to be abating. But suddenly he leaped to his feet, his eyes glittering, and raised his arms with clenched fists and began to shout again.

"Murderers," he shrieked. "You are the real murderers, you who sleep where my voice cannot reach. You with white hands, clean collars, and good manners. You who went to the university and made fortunes by the sweat of others. You who talk about ending poverty and think only of making money. You who talk revolution and love only yourselves. You are Herods and Pilates. You murder by the stroke of a pen, smiling, soft-voiced, too squeamish to bear the sight of blood.

"Caracas stinks of death. Yes, you, Caracas, with your

all-night lights—tourists—advertisements—celebrities—
designer fashions—facelifts and breastlifts and artificial hymens and abortions—presidents in palaces and bishops in palaces—private schools and private planes and private limousines—artists and professors and writers and left-wing politicians—heroin addicts, whiskey addicts, LSD addicts, massage parlors, expensive whores, and money—money—money! City of money—city of killers—city of the accursed!"

Marrero slumped to the ground. His hands scrabbled in the dust, and his eyes bulged like the eyes of a fish. After a while he wept. "City of killers, killers of Christ," he sobbed over and over until his voice died away.

HOLY SATURDAY

XVIII

I‍T WAS MIDMORNING WHEN LUCAS ARRIVED IN CACAGUA to investigate Jesus' early life. The man's story fascinated him and he intended to write it—he felt compelled to write it—even though, as he told himself, its chances of publication were slightly less than nil. A landlady murdered by her husband for sleeping with one of the tenants—that had real human interest. That might make the slick magazines, and the mass-circulation dailies would eat it up. Even an article on Raquel Welch's bikinis—the photographs more than made up for the lack of a story; it made the best kind of filler and was easy to peddle. But slum people made dreary reading: their glamor quotient was zero, and how could they have human interest for readers who never thought of them as human? Stories about slum people didn't sell newspapers, not unless they'd raped one of their betters or committed armed robbery or rioted. The painful struggles of a laborer who lived in a shack in Gramoven and couldn't hold a job but dreamed of changing the world—no editor would touch it, and they'd be right not to because no one would read it. So, then, he was writing it for himself. That was why he was here in Cacagua. He had heard that Jesus was born and grew up here.

He was standing in a village square like a thousand others, with people staring at him from the corner café because he was a stranger and one uniformed policeman yawning in the sun, but the day was mild and calm and he found the place uniquely affecting because the boy Jesus might once have played here. He began to walk.

An elderly woman was coming toward him, and he intercepted her with a deferential tip of his hat and "Good morning, Señora." It was the old people—Jesus' parents' generation or older—who would remember him if anyone would.

"Good morning," she said, smiling and waiting.

"I'm a stranger here. A writer. I'm writing an article about a young man named Jesus Rodriguez. He lives in the Gramoven section of Caracas now, but I'm told he was born here. Have you ever heard of him?"

"No, I don't know who he is," she said, still smiling and looking at the notebook in Lucas' hands.

"Many thanks, anyway. I'll keep asking around."

Her smile became even broader. Lucas wondered if she was simpleminded, but her next words were sensible and to-the-point.

"Señor Sebastian can tell you something, for sure. He knows a lot about everything. He knows more than anyone else in the village."

"And where will I find him?"

"Go straight on up this street till you come to where the buses leave for Araguita. That's where Señor Sebastian lives. He should be at home now. When you come to the buses, ask for him. Everyone here knows him."

He found him sitting in his doorway on an old wooden chair. He was an old man, skeleton-thin and frail, with skin the color of damp earth, but the eyes were keen with intelligence and calm with self-possession. A mountain villager, wise about plants and weather and people.

"Señor Sebastian?"

"At your service."

Lucas smiled to soften the old man's stare.

"I'm collecting information about Jesus Rodriguez. I'm a writer, and I'm thinking of writing about him. I know he was born here, and I'm told that you are the best person to ask for information. I don't know if you know who I'm talking about. Jesus lives in Caracas now, in a poor section. . . ."

"Yes, of course," the old man interrupted, still staring penetratingly at him and obviously a little annoyed that anyone could doubt his power of recollection. "I know very well who you are talking about." He raised a hand in a gesture that commanded Lucas to wait, disappeared inside for a moment, and returned with a second chair. "Sit down. We'll be able to talk more comfortably, and you can take it all down."

The notebook, Lucas realized suddenly, lent him weight and consequence in the village; it confirmed his claim to be a writer.

"So you knew him well?" he asked. Like any good reporter, he knew how to catalyze reminiscence with a flattering and carefully nonspecific question.

"Well, of course. I knew his whole family very well, his father, José and his mother, Maria, and him since he was born. They were all good people. Poor, but good as rain in a dry spell. And what a good worker José was, God rest his soul. Put his whole heart into everything he did, farming or woodworking. He was a fine carpenter, the best, not just a farmer. Did you know that? He was always busy. . . . People always came to him. For carpentry or for charity. Sometimes for both at once. No one ever went away disappointed. He died of fever when the boy was still small. She—Maria— didn't want to marry again, even though she had plenty of offers. They came all the way from Ocumare and even beyond, because she was very pretty and good-tempered and a fine worker. But, I don't know why, she didn't want another husband. She brought up her son alone and always by decent work. Later they moved to Caracas. He goes around the slums helping the worst-off ones. He was always like that, from a child. Gets it from his family. In their house anyone who was hungry could always come and share their meal. José, who is now in heaven, used to say that if God gave them plenty it was so they should give to others. That's why the son is the same way now. He took it in with his mother's milk. His parents made him that way."

Old Sebastian paused and rubbed his hand through his grey hair. He stared at the street for a while, collecting threads of memory.

"Good, all three of them were very good," he said again, nodding to himself. "Some of the best people I've known in my life, and you see how long that's been. So, you from Caracas who know so much and say you are a writer, how old do you think I am?"

Lucas smiled into the old man's eyes.

"I'd say about sixty," he said, without giving it much thought, wanting to get the old man talking about Jesus again.

Señor Sebastian cackled. He looked thoroughly pleased. "Sixty indeed. I'd love to be sixty again. You won't believe me, but I'm much nearer eighty than sixty. You should have seen me when I was sixty! Women ran after me more than after the young men. Sixty! Next month I'll be seventy-seven."

He sat nodding to himself with immense satisfaction. Lucas thought that, anxious as he was to end this digression, he ought to say something complimentary.

"No one would think it. You've certainly worn well. So, you were telling me Jesus was born in one of these houses."

But the old man was still ruminating proudly on his great age.

"Nobody guesses how old I am unless he is a doctor." His eyes were still shining.

"Yes, you're a fine figure of a man. Not many like you," said Lucas. Then he added: "Is the house where Jesus was born near here. Would it be possible to visit it?"

The old man spat with precision and pursed his lips in a silent whistle as he thought.

"No," he said finally. He waited for Lucas to ask him why, but when Lucas simply waited in attentive silence he went on of his own accord. "He wasn't born here. He was born in the fields in a lean-to, near Araguita. His parents were looking for work. They weren't born around here; they came from beyond Altagracia or maybe further south and they were headed for the village but couldn't make it because the mother went into labor. It must have been raining, you know how much it rains around here, there are days that dawn

without a cloud in the sky and before noon everything is
soaking. Well, as I was saying, they were coming to look for
work and Maria went into labor. José fixed up a lean-to using
planks from an abandoned shack. She had the baby there,
right on the cold, wet ground. At least that's what they say. I
didn't see it for myself. Eustaquio who was minding cows up
there found them and gave them some warm milk straight
from the udder. He came back with all sorts of stories: that he
heard strange music and saw all kinds of visions, but none of
us believed him because Eustaquio is a great story-teller and
he gets so carried away by his own stories that he believes
them himself, and besides he's a great believer in spirits and
ghosts and such like. Not that I don't believe in them myself,
because there are spirits, yes there are. The spirit of my son
Melquiades is haunting my own house. He died about three
months ago from an accident, and it seems he hasn't been
able to rest yet. He won't let my poor daughter-in-law—that's
Felipa, his wife—sleep. He comes and chokes her and says
he's going to take her away. We'll have to have the priest
come and sprinkle holy water. Raimundo the medicine man,
he came three times and couldn't do a thing, the spirit is too
strong for him. Yes, we'll have to call the priest to see if he
can get rid of the spirit so poor Felipa can sleep in peace.
Sometimes priests have a lot of power over these spirits."

Old Sebastian raised his eyes and rubbed his scalp again.
He seemed to be searching for the lost thread of his thoughts.
He looked at Lucas as if asking for help. Then he said: "But I
don't remember what I was telling you about. . . ."

"You were talking about Eustaquio. You said he found
them and that. . . ."

"Ah yes, I remember now," interrupted the old man, and
his eyes were bright again. "Nobody believed him about the
apparitions and the music, but it's true that Jesus was born up
there on the mountain in pouring rain. In fact Eustaquio was
very fond of him when he was young. Said he was marked out
to be great in some way. He brought him pebbles, colored
stones from the river . . . you know, all sorts of things that
children loved so much when there weren't so many toys

like there are now. When Jesus grew older Eustaquio used to take him up the mountain and let him sit on the bullocks, teach him songs, and give him milk fresh from the cow."

"And would it be possible for me to talk to Eustaquio?" interrupted Lucas.

"Eustaquio is dead now, God and the Virgin rest his soul. He died many years ago. Snakebite. He was bitten by a bushmaster that must have been full of poison because it bit him and Eustaquio just fell right down in a dead faint. My friend Faustino who was with him when he was bitten made a cut where the bite was and tried to suck out the poison but it was no good. He died the same day without ever waking up. He didn't suffer, but he didn't get to say good-bye to his friends either. I saw how Jesus cried at his funeral. I thought the boy would die of crying so much. Because they were very fond of each other. . . ."

"Has Jesus ever been back here since he left?"

"Yes, of course. He comes back a lot. He visits us and talks to us about how things should be. Sometimes he tells us stories to explain his ideas. He says we must stick to our own ways and not take up with the things we see on television because they are killing Venezuela, giving it over to the Yankees without us noticing that it's happening. He says it's like a worm inside a fruit: The worm eats away the inside, but from the outside the fruit still looks beautiful. He tells the farmers they should organize themselves into cooperatives so the middlemen can't rob them coming and going, which they do now, and he's right. He even tells them they should organize to own the land that they work, because, he says, the landlords get rich off their work and it's not right. He's right about that too. He says God made us all equal, all his children, and that's why we must demand our rights and we must not let anyone trample on us as if we were less human than the rich. The landlords don't like his ideas, mostly; they say he is a Communist and some of them even threaten him with the police. But for me this is not communism but the simple truth, because when God came on earth he said that we were all equal."

While the old man was speaking, Lucas was conscious only of his story. Now that he had stopped, the street noises and increasing humidity intruded oppressively on his awareness. He waited for the old man to rouse himself again.

"Now I'll tell you a very good story that he told us. I remember it very well. It explains about capitalism and private property and how wrong it is and what it does to people like us. It's a good story. He said that once there was a very dry village, without any water at all. The people who lived on it were dying of thirst and they went to look for water. Finally after a long search some of them found water and said it belonged to them and stored it in a reservoir. These were called capitalists. The other people of the village who hadn't found any water yet were dying of thirst so they went to ask the capitalists, 'Please give us a little water.' But the capitalists said, 'Don't be stupid. Do you think we are fools or something? Why should we give you our water, that we found, for nothing? You want water, do you? Well, work for us and then we'll give you water.' The people had to accept because they were parched with thirst. So the capitalists set the people to work. They made some look for more water and some dig wells and some carry the water to a tank that they called a market. And the capitalists said to the people: 'Listen, for each keg of water you carry to the store we'll give you one bolivar, and for each keg of water you take from the store to drink you must give us two bolivars." The people didn't understand this very well and anyway they were very thirsty, so they said all right. And that's how it was: They got one bolivar for each keg of water they carried to the tank and paid two bolivars for each keg of water they took out of the tank.

"But finally, after a long time, the tank was full to overflowing, because for each keg of water the people put in they could only pay to take out half a keg for themselves. And another reason the tank overflowed was that although the capitalists who didn't work drank all the water they wanted, there were few of them and they couldn't use up what the people couldn't afford. Then the capitalists, who were very

clever, said to the people: 'Don't bring any more water because the tank is full to overflowing. We have an economic
crisis. Wait and be patient and we'll see how we can get over
it.'"

"So there was unemployment."

"Now that the people had no money to buy water because
they were out of work, the owners started a big advertising
campaign for water in the papers and on television.
Everywhere there were advertisements saying: DRINK
WATER. DRINK WATER. IF YOU WANT TO BE
HEALTHY AND STRONG DRINK WATER FROM OUR
STORE. IF YOU WANT TO HAVE AN IRRESISTIBLE
BODY DRINK MORE AND MORE WATER. They even
photographed beautiful girls in bikinis beside the water tank
and on television the girls said in seductive voices that their
beauty came from drinking or bathing in this water.

"But the people could not buy water because they had no
work. They were getting thirstier and thirstier, because the
capitalists had taken over all the springs and streams and
even the rain barrels. Then the village people said: 'This
stinks! The tank is overflowing and we and our children are
dying of thirst. It they don't give us water we're dead!'

"And the capitalists didn't let them come near the water
because they said it was private property, and they even
hired armed guards to protect it. Where did they get these
guards? The guards were village people just like the others,
but the capitalists gave them water as pay for being guards,
so they were guards. About the people dying of thirst the
capitalists said 'business is business' and 'you can't be sentimental in business.'

"But advertising couldn't make people buy water when
they had no money to buy it with, and when the money
stopped coming in the capitalists began to worry. As they
saw it, they weren't making any more money because there
was too much water. So they called in the big-mouth experts
who told them their problem was 'overproduction,' 'excess
accumulation,' which was caused by world inflation. The
capitalists put these reasons in their newspapers and told the

experts to explain them to the people. But the people didn't understand. What they did understand was that none of these highbrow words would make them any less thirsty. So they threatened to lynch the experts and the experts ran back to the capitalists terrified. But the capitalists forced them to go back to the village and explain overproduction and inflation again to the people; that's what they were paying them for. So the experts and the economists and the planners tried every which way to convince the people that they had no water because there was too much water and that there was nothing they could do but die of thirst because there was too much water. The people threw stones at them so that they ran away. When they came again they were protected by the army. There were clashes, and some of the soldiers and village men were hurt. None of the capitalists, none of the experts ever got hurt.

"Then when the capitalists saw that the experts were getting nowhere and the people were getting desperate and maybe dangerous, they called in the priests to try and calm the people down. Some of the priests refused and even tried to organize the people to take over the water tank and collect and distribute the water themselves, but most of the priests went to the village and preached to the people that this great thirst was a trial sent by God and that if they died of thirst they would go to heaven where there was no more thirst, no more work, and no more capitalists.

"But the people drove out these lying priests too, and the capitalists became frightened, so they began to give out tiny cupfuls of water to the thirsty people. They gave out this water with much boasting about their good Christian hearts, but these cups of water were very small, and besides, they were charity, and most of the people found them bitter to the taste.

"Now the store of water was getting lower, because the capitalists not only drank all the water they wanted but they also built swimming pools and fish ponds and fountains in their gardens to enjoy themselves more. When they saw the water was running out, they said the crisis was over and

hired the people to carry water again. But now they paid
three bolivars for every keg taken out. They said it wasn't
that they were making more money but that inflation had
raised the cost of production and maintenance. Some of them
said too that if the water seemed too expensive to the people
they needn't buy it. And the people started work again so as
not to die of thirst, and bought what little water they could
with their wages.

"And again the tank filled to overflowing. Oh, yes, and I
forgot to tell you that now the capitalists put many people to
work building canals so that the water could flow directly
from the springs to the storage tanks and then they wouldn't
need any more water carriers.

"Then came the agitators. Most of these men didn't work
or go thirsty. They always seemed to have enough money for
water. They made fiery speeches to the people about freeing
themselves from slavery to the capitalists. Some of them
were arrested and some were even killed by the capitalists,
but a lot of them disappeared when things got rough and left
the people holding the bag. And nothing much changed.

"But the more intelligent people began to realize that
even though the agitators had their own fish to fry, what they
said about the capitalists was true: They really were heart-
less exploiters who were living high on other people's work
and misery and didn't want anything to change. These
people began to see that television and newspapers only said
what the capitalists wanted, because they were owned by
them: lies to confuse and frighten the people and keep them
down forever. They began to understand that the more they
worked the poorer they would be, as long as the capitalists
could pay them one bolivar a keg of water and charge them
three bolivars a keg. They saw that this difference, which the
capitalists called 'profit' or 'return,' was plain robbery, and it
would go on for as long as it was up to the capitalists to decide
how much to pay and how much to charge. They tried to
make their friends understand all this too, but at first nobody
took much notice of them. First because they had gotten
used to their situation and thought of it as normal and second

because the newspapers, television, and even their priests told them that people who talked against capitalists were 'resentful,' 'embittered,' and even 'crazy fools' who were saying all this stuff to betray their country to some very bad people, Russians or something, who would come and close down all the churches and kill the priests and anyone who had statues of saints at home and even take away their children. It would be like Cuba, where there was no food, no clothes, nothing, and that's why all the people wanted to get out.

"That was at first. But the longer people worked the poorer and more miserable they got, and the richer the capitalists got, and little by little more and more people were understanding the truth. They understood that the remedy was to organize themselves to get rid of the capitalists, who did no work, but only bossed them and got fat by other people's labor. They understood that if they shared the work and the water, living like brothers and sisters, no one would be thirsty and the water tank would never overflow. If there was water to spare after everyone had enough they could build swimming pools for everyone to swim in, not just a few people. Then the people started choosing leaders from among themselves, people smart enough to lead them who would love them instead of exploiting them, because they would not be masters but like elder brothers and sisters.

"And the people began to do all this. But by now the capitalists were so rich that they had a large and powerful army. And the capitalists sent their army against the people and even asked capitalists from other countries to send their armies to help. But in the end the people won, because there were so many of them and because they were fighting for themselves, not for pay. And they shared the work and shared the water and everyone had plenty. And they even went to the capitalists and invited them to join in the new life of equality, saying they had nothing against them personally but only against how they used to treat people. But they also said that if they saw the capitalists trying to go back to their old ways they would smash them.

"And nobody was ever thirsty again in that land, or hungry or cold. And every man called his companion brother and every woman called her companion sister. Because they all lived like brothers and sisters in love and peace."

The old man finished his story in a voice like a trumpet call. His eyes were shining at the vision he had conjured up.

"That's the way he talks to us when he comes. He speaks plainly and we all understand. He tells us wonderful stories like that one, and I keep them in my heart."

Old Sebastian's voice was suddenly hoarse. He had a coughing fit, and then he spat several times. Lucas waited, but he said no more.

"They say Jesus the Christ many years ago spoke to people like that," said Lucas after a while.

The old man smiled contentedly at the comparison. "All Jesuses are the same," he said hoarsely.

XIX

Luis yawned noisily and opened his eyes. The light was bright yellow and he shut them again at once. He heard the sea nearby but did not look at it. He lay a long while, thinking nothing, rocking drowsily in his hammock. He wondered whether he felt thirsty, and although he wasn't sure he called out for a "very cold beer." It came at once, in a tall mug on a tray, brought by Ignacia, the black servant who waited on them when they came to the beach.

"How lazy the young master is," said Ignacia in her voice like rushing waters.

Luis opened his eyes and looked into her face, conscious of being "the young master."

"Yes, and nothing gets rid of it better than a woman under you."

Ignacia laughed nervously.

"Oh, what a nerve you have," she said.

"Nerve? Why? Isn't it true that women are the cure for laziness?"

"Yes, that's true," said Ignacia with a guileless smile and went back to the kitchen.

Luis took a long draught of beer that made his eyes water. He began to think about Ignacia—what she would be like as a "cure for laziness." If he just laid a hand on her she would probably start trembling like a bitch in heat, and he could have her right there on the kitchen floor, a few yards away from the room where his parents were taking their siesta. Blacks were always ready; she wouldn't need any coaxing.

The idea took hold of him, and he lay mulling it over. Maybe it would be even more fun to play with her, excite her, get her hot, and then just walk away and leave her.

He climbed out of the hammock and headed for the kitchen. Ignacia was mopping the floor.

"I've come for you to cure my laziness."

Ignacia did not look at him. She went on working as if she hadn't heard. Luis persisted. "You're supposed to do things for me. I want you to cure my laziness. You'll enjoy it."

Ignacia glanced at him. Her eyes were bright and Luis thought it must be with desire.

"Don't say such things, sir," she said. Her voice shook.

Luis went closer to her. "Stop pretending! You want to. I can see it in your face."

"You are quite mistaken, sir. I have a husband and children."

Luis laughed.

"Come on, Ignacia, don't start playing respectable with me. It's not as if you people took marriage seriously. . . . How many tourists have you gone with on the beach? Or do you only do it with other blacks?"

Ignacia stopped mopping and stared at him. She looked furious, but her voice was even and toneless: "You are offending me, sir."

Luis was puzzled. Things weren't supposed to take this turn. He had to have her now or admit defeat at the hands of a menial. How to convince her?

"I'll give you money," he said pressingly. "You can earn in a minute what you earn in a month. And without doing any work, just enjoying yourself."

"I've already told you, sir, that you are quite mistaken. I am not a bad woman." She picked up her mop and bucket and, leaving the floor half-done, went out of the room in silence.

This was humiliating! Worst of all, he didn't know what to do. How could such a woman, ugly and ignorant and immoral—they were all immoral—refuse a young man like himself? She had even refused money (although he hadn't actually intended to pay her)! The stupid—! Wasn't two minutes on the floor with him better than hours of cleaning floors! Suddenly he felt afraid. What if she told her husband? These people all carried switchblades and thought nothing of using them! He shuddered and felt nauseous.

"Relax!" he told himself. "She won't tell him because she has everything to lose. We'd fire her, and she needs her job. And even if she did tell her husband he wouldn't dare do anything against a Rengifo. All he'd do, probably, is get mad and slap her around. Anyway I could deny it all or say it was a joke."

He felt better, opened himself another beer, and considered what to do. He thought of going down to the beach, but it was too hot at this time of day. He went back to the hammock and lay down, rocking a little, sipping beer without feeling thirsty, feeling intolerably bored. He went into the living room and put on a Bee-Gees record, but the music, which he had thought he liked, grated on his nerves. He tried several more records, tore each one off the turntable in disgust, and finally broke the last one into six pieces and stamped out, leaving the pieces on the floor.

He took the car and drove round El Playon, letting the breeze whip his face. He thought he might go into Caracas to see Elizabeth. He would put his arms around her, tell her he loved her, that he hadn't been able to stand it without her, and she would let him do anything he wanted. But afterward, when they had finished, the weariness and boredom would still be there, waiting, along with the truth that made his life unbearable: He was incapable of loving anybody. He gave up the idea of going to Caracas—it seemed too much bother to go home, get dressed, tell his parents he was going to Caracas, and then spend all those hours driving.

"What's the point? I'll feel the same in Caracas as I do here. No place makes any difference." He drove the car toward the bridge, but before he came to it he turned off onto a dirt track that led down to the river. He found a place where the earth was soft and lay down there, pretending it was Elizabeth's body, but at the moment of climax Elizabeth turned into black Ignacia.

Afterward he lay on the ground, reluctant to open his eyes,

filled with an overwhelming sadness. He saw his empty, intolerable life, aimless, without dreams, not worth the trouble of living. Car rides with friends, parties, easy girls, continual lies to Elizabeth, the dreary routine of "having fun." . . . His self-loathing became anguish. And he would go on like that, willy-nilly, hating his life but without the strength to change it. And he remembered again how once he had tried to live differently. It was during the final year of college, when he began to feel the futility of his life and felt a great urge to change it. He did not want to become like his father, a slave to his shares and his bank notes, worrying over the fluctuations of the stock market, cellulitis, whiskey, and his checkbook. His friend Juan (whom he hadn't seen for how long now?) told him about Jesus and the work they were doing in the slums. It had sounded inspiring, and one afternoon he went up the hill to Gramoven to talk to Jesus.

"I want to do something worthwhile with my life," Luis told him. "I'm so bored. I want to work with you for the people."

Jesus had just finished work. He looked very tired. Still he looked searchingly at Luis and smiled.

"This is a hard life," he said.

"I'd still like to try."

"If you really want to join us, leave your house and your money, sell whatever is yours and give the money to the poor, and come and live with me."

That he had not expected! To help the poor was noble. To be one of them was a fearful and horrible prospect.

"I'll come back another day," he said quickly.

He did not go back again.

XX

J UDAS WALKED FASTER AND FASTER, but the thoughts that he was fleeing from kept grim pace with him. Could Señora Remedios have been telling the truth? Bah! She was a malicious old woman! But then Jesus had condemned himself by his own words last night at supper in Madalena's house. Out of his own mouth he stood exposed as a terrorist. What more proof did he want? It wasn't proofs he lacked but the courage to do his duty. He was a coward. But what should he, Judas, do? Wasn't it enough to break with Jesus and persuade others to do the same? But would they take any notice? By not warning the authorities, wasn't he leaving Jesus free to agitate and mislead the people and ultimately lead them to violence and destruction?

He had an instant's lurid vision of hordes of slum-dwellers descending upon the center of Caracas in an orgy of looting, burning, and killing. He saw the city after they had finished with it: smoldering and lifeless.

He found himself at his house but kept on walking, wondering mirthlessly if he could walk till he reached nowhere. He passed some boys making straw men for the "burning of Judas" the next day.

"Hey, shopkeeper! Tomorrow we're going to burn Pinochet. What do you think? Can you think of any other good Judases?"

The voice seemed to come from another planet. Judas shook his head and smiled vaguely.

143

"Why do we need a straw man? We've got a real flesh-and-blood Judas here," joked one of the boys. "Let's burn him."

Some of them laughed. Judas tore himself away from them, almost running. Could that kid see into his thoughts, to call him a "flesh-and-blood Judas" like that?

"Where are you going, Judas? We were only joking. You're running as if the devil was after you. Come back."

The boys' words fell behind him into the darkness.

He found himself back at his shop and stopped. His inchoate anguish was forming into an idea, a resolution: He would denounce him. Christ himself required this of him. Christ would give him the strength to do it.

He breathed deeply, then smiled, feeling like a hunted creature whose pursuers had given up the chase. "No one can serve two masters," he told himself. "I chose Christ and now I won't look back. I'll do my duty. If I'm mistaken about him, the authorities will know it and no harm will be done."

The boys making the straw men did not see him going by again.

"I have come to lodge a complaint against the citizen Jesus Rodriguez." Although he had practiced saying it over and over, even out loud, Judas could not keep his voice from trembling.

The policeman looked at him wearily over a mug of lukewarm coffee.

"Name and identity card?" he asked, setting down the cup and reaching for a pen.

"Judas Martinez." His brain was whirling again, and his heart lurching against his ribs. The policeman wrote with nerve-wracking slowness. Where did they find these illiterates?

"Well?" The policeman looked at him again without the slightest interest.

"He is a communist activist."

The policeman looked bored and annoyed. "Even though it's a disgrace, the communist party is legal," he said.

"It's not that. You see, he's a dangerous man." Judas flushed and began to sweat. The policeman's indifference was making him feel like a fool. He began to feel sorry he had come.

"We can't arrest anyone just for 'being dangerous,'" replied the policeman. "Have you no specific charge to make?"

"He took part in the kidnapping of the Ramirez brothers," Judas said at last, almost yelling the words.

The boredom vanished from the bored face behind the desk.

"Wait a moment," the policeman said.

He dialed a telephone number, keeping his eyes on Judas all the while.

"I have here a citizen who has some extremely interesting and important information."

When he hung up he was smiling grimly, and it was with a clumsy, unpracticed courtesy that he ushered Judas into an inner office and bade him sit down.

The man's sudden change in manner made Judas realize at last that he had done something irreparable. It was in their hands now. He could not stop it if he tried. He sat down.

He could not tell how long he had been there when a police officer entered the room.

He smiled at Judas, but he did not introduce himself. "Well, what is this information you have for us?"

"It's about Jesus Rodriguez. He took part in the kidnapping of the Ramirez brothers."

The officer's expression remained noncommittal. He seemed to be waiting for Judas to continue, but when Judas seemed at a loss for words, he prompted him: "Isn't he the fellow who goes around causing trouble in the slums?"

"Yes, yes, and in the factories. He's been fired from quite a few jobs," said Judas, relieved to know that the police already knew something incriminating about Jesus' activities.

"We have had several complaints about him," continued the officer, "but none as serious as yours. But tell me, how did you come by this information?"

Judas cleared his throat. He felt flushed, and wondered if the officer would doubt his evidence because of it.

"We live in the same neighborhood. I know him well. I've been a friend of his for quite a while."

The officer barely smiled.

"And why, if you are his friend, have you decided to come here and lay such a serious charge against him?"

Judas looked him in the face. "For the good of the country and because my faith requires it." He had intended to sound firm, but in his own ears it came out sounding merely too loud.

The officer nodded slightly.

"Do you know if he usually goes about armed?" he asked then, in a much more professional tone.

"No, I don't know that he does," said Judas. "But still I don't think it would be wise to arrest him in his own neighborhood. A lot of people there would fight to protect him." He was silent a moment, looking at his fingernails, and then raised his eyes and said, "Tonight he has gone with his mother to the cathedral." Then, as if realizing that such behavior did not fit a communist agitator and terrorist, he added quickly, "You know, she is a widow, an old lady now, and very devout."

"What you've told us is very useful," said the officer briskly. "Can you give us a detailed description of him?"

"He is dark, tall, thirty-three years old, strongly built. . . . But he will certainly be among friends. If you like, I will go up to him and greet him. Then you will be sure of your identification."

The officer stared at him. Judas felt his face crumpling under that appraising stare; he looked away, then glanced back imploringly several times, begging the officer to take his eyes off him.

"You really hate him, don't you?" It was more a statement than a question.

"No. I don't know," Judas said without looking at him. And then he added, sounding surprised and hurt: "I always thought I liked him."

Again the bells rang out in the Caracas night, festive and triumphant and punctuated by the crackle of fireworks. The congregation was emerging slowly from the cathedral, looking joyful, feeling triumphant. The air was murmurous with greetings: "Happy Easter," "Christ is risen."

Judas came forward out of the night toward the group of Jesus, his mother, Madalena, and Juan.

"Happy Easter," he said and clasped Jesus on the shoulder without looking at him.

"Hello, Judas. Happy Easter. How are you? Look, come with us and have some cakes."

"Thanks, but I'm in a hurry. I was just passing and saw you."

He hastened away without greeting any of the others.

"He's still angry," said Madalena and looked at Jesus.

"He'll soon get over it," answered Jesus and began walking, with his hand on his mother's shoulder.

Suddenly two strange men stood blocking their way.

"Jesus Rodriguez?"

"Yes?"

"Come with us."

He felt the muzzle of a revolver in his back. His mother was holding his arm tightly with both hands.

"Wait for me at home, mama."

"I stay with you."

They pried her hands loose and pushed him into a parked car.

"The rest of you, get lost!" said one of the men as the engine started.

"What happened, mum?" asked a wide-eyed child.

"Probably plainclothesmen arresting a pickpocket."

"And why are the bells ringing so loud, mum?"

"Jesus has risen, child. This is the greatest night of the year."

EPILOGUE

(This epilogue was written by the journalist Lucas Cedeño and published in a Caracas newspaper some weeks after the events just narrated.)

DISAPPEARANCE OF JESUS OF GRAMOVEN STILL AN UNSOLVED MYSTERY—Twenty-three days later there is still no clue to his whereabouts. The mystery surrounding the disappearance of Gramoven is still unsolved, and there seems to be no prospect of its solution in the near future. The authorities continue to deny any knowledge of the case. They interpret the statements of the victim's mother and friends who were present at the events of the night of Saturday, April 20, as indicating that he was kidnapped by a gang of bandits or paid gunmen. They repeat, however, that the law enforcement agents are doing all they can to discover Jesus' whereabouts and arrest his abductors. As is well known, the statements of Jesus' mother, a young man called Juan, and a neighbor known as Madalena, all agree that on the night of April 20th, just after they had come from midnight mass at the cathedral church, as they approached Marron corner two men in civilian clothing approached Jesus Rodriguez, popular leader of Gramoven, kidnapped him at pistol point, and drove off with him in an unmarked car whose license number they were too surprised and shaken to note. That was the last time Jesus Rodriguez was seen, and nothing more is known about his disappearance.

Two days after Jesus Rodriguez's disappearance his friend Judas Martinez committed suicide. A woman who happened to witness his suicide declared that just before he threw himself from one of the apartment buildings, Judas

149

screamed, "Jesus is dead, and I am guilty! I betrayed him!"
The witness reports, however, that Sr. Martinez appeared
drunk or distraught or both. He died without revealing to
whom he had betrayed him.

Friends of the two men state that they had recently quar-
relled and think that it must have been these quarrels that
led Judas to plot Jesus' death by pointing him out to personal
enemies. It is well known that Jesus' ideas had earned him
many enemies. This theory is corroborated by the statement
of witnesses that a few moments before the kidnapping
Judas had walked up to Jesus, greeted him, and patted him
on the shoulder. He had looked nervous and left quickly
despite an invitation to join the group. These details strongly
suggest that the gunmen were hired killers to whom Jesus
was a stranger and to whom, therefore, Judas had to point
him out. Some people have suggested that Judas himself
hired the gunmen, but those who knew him best insist that
such an act was not in his character, no matter how bitter his
recent disagreements with Jesus might have been. Even
more conclusive is the argument that hired killers usually
charge much more than a neighborhood shopkeeper could
ever afford to pay. Moreover, his cry of "I betrayed him!"
further supports the thesis that Judas, in a fit of anger, merely
fingered Jesus for other, more powerful enemies who then
eliminated him. Had Judas hired the killer himself, he
would have been more likely to cry out, "I killed him," than
"I betrayed him." The writer has no clear information on the
disagreements that lately separated Judas and Jesus. It is to
be suspected that they were related to the process of
consciousness-raising being undertaken by Jesus among his
neighbors and co-workers. Judas, a militant Christian of a
preconciliar cast, probably found this process too "revolutionary."

All the same, the mystery remains. Who could have
wanted Jesus dead? Or at least out of the way, for his death is
only a presumption—his body has not been found. To whom
and why did Judas Martinez betray him? What did the kid-
nappers do with him?

It is known that a few days before his kidnapping Jesus

Rodriguez was fired from Linares Industries, where he had been employed as a laborer, but the police deny that this dismissal has any connection with his disappearance. On the other hand Jesus' neighbors and co-workers are skeptical of all official statements about the kidnapping. Although they will not say so openly, they suspect that certain elements in government felt sufficiently threatened by Jesus' credo of justice and brotherhood, and by his great personal popularity, to eliminate him. Spokesmen for various left-wing parties demand that this possibility be thoroughly investigated, but if the government is indeed involved, it is unlikely to bring evidence against itself. The major newspapers and journals, apart from publishing the official police hypothesis that Jesus was done away with by professional criminals for "personal reasons," have generally ignored the story.

Amid this climate of uncertainty and suspicion, and despite the sorrow felt by Jesus' friends, a new spirit is entering their lives. They talk of carrying out Jesus' ideas in his name. Some even say that Jesus is not dead, that he lives among them because he has left them the example of his life and ideals to help them in their struggles.

Also from Orbis . . .

BUHLMANN, Walbert, O.F.M. Cap.
THE COMING OF THE THIRD CHURCH
An Analysis of the Present and Future of the Church

by Walbert Buhlmann, O.F.M. Cap.
"Karl Rahner called this the best book of the year, Sister Margaret Brennan, IHM, the book of the decade. It is both." *Commonweal*
Buhlmann "presents a broad survey of current trends that he has observed and studied throughout the world. In addition he has ventured to present some bold predictions about the future in the areas of ecclesiology and missiology." *Worldmission*
"His recommendations are on the whole simply magnificent and vital. The richness of the book in factual information and recommendations is a tribute to the author's deep and longlasting concern about the real mission of the church." *Religious Book Review*
"When reviewing books for *Missionalia* I try to refrain from referring to any as 'required reading for everybody.' This book is an exception. I cannot but urge each and everyone of our subscribers to read it, and to read it carefully." *Missionalia*
"If you have time and money this year for only one serious book, *The Coming of the Third Church* is the one to purchase and study with an open mind and a sincere heart. Comparisons are always odious but this is easily the best Catholic book in English that I have come across this year." *Priests USA*
"A magnificent theological analysis of the contemporary missionary task." *The Christian Century*

ISBN 0-88344-069-5 CIP
ISBN 0-88344-070-9

Cloth $12.95
Paper $6.95

GUTIERREZ, Gustavo
A THEOLOGY OF LIBERATION
"This is one of the most acute and the most readable theological essays of today on the meaning and mission of the Church." *Catholic Library World*
"Rarely does one find such a happy fusion of gospel content and contemporary relevance." *The Lutheran Standard*

ISBN 0-88344-477-1
ISBN 0-88344-478-X

Cloth $7.95
Paper $4.95

PAOLI, Arturo
FREEDOM TO BE FREE

"A timely, interesting, and unusual book on the theology of liberation, revolution, and peacemaking, as reflected in the thought of an activist. Paoli is a member of the Congregation of the Little Brothers at Fortin Olmos in Argentina. He came to realize that freedom of the individual and of society is the Gospel message, proclaimed by Christ in his life, death and resurrection. Paoli deals with freedom in all its dimensions and manifestations. Biblical thought, especially that of St. Paul, is the cornerstone of the author's thesis. Paoli argues that an updating by the Church in Latin America is urgent if she is to confront contemporary issues successfully. In this urgency lies the book's great value. The English translation is welcome. Recommended for courses on social action or peace as well as in religion." *Choice*

"Full of eye-opening reflections on how Jesus liberated man through poverty, the Cross, the Eucharist and prayer." *America*
ISBN 0-88344-143-8   *311pp. Paper $4.95*

CARDENAL, Ernesto
THE GOSPEL IN SOLENTINAME

"Farmers and fishermen in a remote village in Nicaragua join their priest for dialogues on Bible verses. The dialoguers discover Jesus as the liberator come to deliver *them* from oppression, inequality, and injustice imposed by a rich, exploitive class: they identify Herod as dictator Somoza. Their vision of the Kingdom of God on earth impels them toward political revolution. This is 'Marxian Christianity' not as abstract theory but gropingly, movingly articulated by poor people. Highly recommended to confront the complacent with the stark realities of religious and political consciousness in the Third World." *Library Journal*

The colorful Nicaraguan country church, where the fishermen and farmers and their families gathered for the liturgy, is now a military barracks. In October 1977, the soldiers of the Somoza regime burned the houses of the islanders and vandalized the library and other facilities of this world famous Christian community. Many lost their lives, others are in hiding. This is the price they are paying for being faithful to the Gospel in their struggle against oppression and corruption.
ISBN 0-88344-170-5   *Paper $4.95*